# MINE TONIGHT

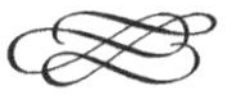

## CHRISTINA C JONES

*Mine Tonight*

*Christina C. Jones*

# AUTHOR'S NOTE

*I want to dedicate this to the wonderful, awesome, magnificent, spectacular members of #TeamCCJ on Facebook. We've had so much fun, and I've learned so much in just these few short weeks. Your encouragement means so, so much, and I'm so, so grateful!*

*This was fun.*
*This was really, really fun.*
*This was a project I embarked on to help me past a writing slump, and also to work on my skills at writing intimate scenes.*
*Happy reading!*

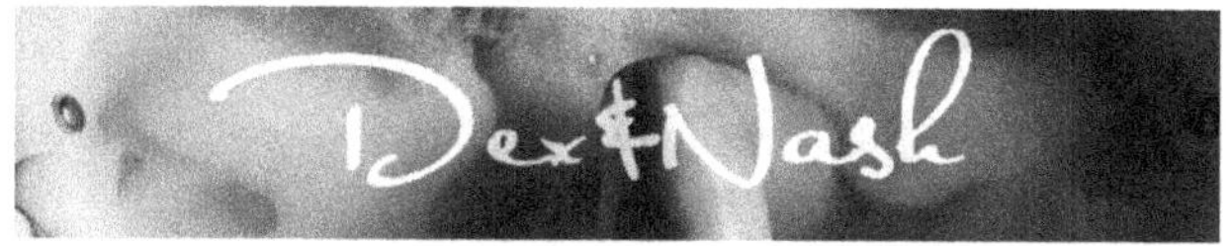

"*W*hat would you do if I told you to take off your clothes?"

In the mirrored wall of the elevator, I watched his face, waiting for an answer. His mouth twitched, trying not to smile, showing the brief flash of a dimple just above the neatly trimmed edge of his low beard. I caught the subtle shake of his head, the suppressed laughter, and then, in the mirror, he met my eyes, but said nothing.

He thought I was playing.

"Answer the question." I turned to face him as we passed the 26th floor. Even in my four inch heels, I had to look up to meet his eyes – deep, warm pools of rich brown, marbled and edged with darker black. The kind of eyes you didn't want to look away from, so I didn't. "If I told you to get naked right now, and fuck me... what would you do?"

His Adam's apple bobbed as he swallowed hard, but his face didn't change. He kept his face impassive and professional, exactly what he was supposed to do when faced with impropriety. He was paid to hear nothing, see nothing, say nothing, feel nothing, only protect. *Not* entertain my lack of decorum.

"*Dexter*," I said, in a distinctly scolding tone that made his jaw twitch. "Don't ignore me. What would you do?"

"Nothing."

I narrowed my eyes. Not because of his answer, but because of the way the deep rumble of his voice caressed my skin, touching me in places I wanted *him* to touch. Places I'd always wanted him to touch, but he'd refused.

But that was then. This was *now*. And now… things were different.

Dexter had always been fine as hell. He had deep, rich, lusciously smooth dark brown skin, so flawless that I didn't even mind the cliché when my brain connected it to a bar of chocolate. Lush, full lips, perfectly sculpted nose, and those damned sleepy, heavy-lidded eyes I couldn't look away from.

"But I'm your boss," I said, stepping close enough to be surrounded in the spicy, clean scent of his cologne. "You're supposed to do what I tell you. *Anything* I tell you."

One corner of his mouth tipped into a smirk. "You're thinking of a slave."

"That's what I pay you to be, right?"

His smirk dropped as he moved to a new position, standing between me and the elevator doors as we passed the 53rd floor. His hand went to the sleek black gun strapped to his waist, ready to fire if necessary, and he didn't answer my question.

I glared at his back. His shoulders were wide and strong, and underneath that suit, I knew he was corded with muscles that would undoubtedly feel good under my fingers as I dug my nails into his back. Thick, and strong… the body of a grown assed man.

"You'd take a bullet for me, right?" Our eyes met in the mirror, and he said nothing, but we both knew the answer was yes. He would take a bullet, or five, or fifty, because it was dictated by the terms of his employment. "So you're saying you'd take a bullet for me, but fucking me would be unreasonable?"

I rolled my eyes as the elevator doors opened and he strode out, checking for anyone who didn't belong before he motioned for me to join him, and still not answering the damned question. Sucking my teeth, I walked in front of him, which I was sure broke some sort of protocol, but whatever. I was slipping a hand in my purse to pull out my key card when strong fingers circled my forearm with just enough pressure to hold me in place.

"Mrs. Haley…" his voice was low, dangerous, edged with enough annoyance that I had to fight back a smile, hiding the joy I felt at getting under his skin. "I'm going to have to ask you to follow proper procedure ma'am."

"And if I don't?" I challenged, hoping that my defiance would wear even further on his nerves.

He ran his tongue over his teeth. "Then I'll put your drunk ass over my shoulder, and just carry you inside."

"I'm not drunk." I snatched away from his grip, then immediately stumbled on my heels like a baby giraffe. I would have been a mess of long legs on the floor if it wasn't for Dexter's swift action. Instead, I was caught up in his arms.

He grinned – a phenomenon I'd rarely seen, because he was usually Mr. Serious when it came to me – showing off perfect teeth and ·even more perfect dimples. From dangerous sexy to adorable sexy… my panties were wet either way.

"*Not* drunk huh?" he asked, pulling me up and holding me steady.

I looked down at the way he was holding me, clutched up

against his body, then grinned right back. "*Not* going to fuck me, huh?"

All night, my breasts had been threatening to spill out of my daring dress, and now they were pressed against him. The dress was white, strapless, and curve hugging, with a sweetheart neckline… unapologetically sexy, but undoubtedly appropriate for the event I'd just left. *My* event.

I approached the grand opening of a hotel with the same energy and excitement some women reserved for weddings. Everything had to be perfect, down to the last detail. Don't bring me lime when I asked for citron, no gray when I asked for silver. Twenty-two roses at every centerpiece, not nineteen, or twenty-five.

Reputation as a hard-ass be damned, when something had my name on it, it had to be right. And this event, the grand opening of my stepfather's twenty-second luxury hotel in the United States… I'd gotten it right.

It was perfect.

From the flawlessly coordinated wait staff to the immaculately polished chandeliers – not a blown bulb in sight— this event was the epitome of what I could do, an impeccable example of my talent… and it gave me no joy. As beautiful as everything was, all I could think about was getting the hell out of there, so that's what I decided to do.

I moved gracefully around the room on four-inch heels, smiling at and speaking to potential investors and guests while avoiding contact with any members of my family. Malcolm Armstrong– the stepfather I mentioned – was a stickler for professionalism and customer service, and had ground that principle into my brothers and me from an early age. *Best foot forward,* I could practically hear him saying in my ear. Even when you were going through a personal crisis.

So I was handling it.

If nothing else, I was a good actress, so I pretended everything was perfectly fine, until I couldn't. Somewhere around the second pass of crab cakes, I decided I was leaving. The vibrant crowd was stifling, the overhead lights were blinding, and the heavy, pulsing music from the live jazz band was giving me a headache.

No.

*Worsening* my headache.

If I were going to give credit for my discomfort to any one thing, it would be the fact that I felt obligated to attend this little shindig at all. But it wasn't always like that. Once upon a time, I would have thrived at such an event. At *my* event.

But not tonight.

All I wanted to do was get away from here. I lived upstairs, in one of the permanent residence suites, but I had no desire to be there, not really. I just wanted to be… away.

I handed out a few more smiles, then edged myself away from the crowd. My destination – the short hall that led to the double-door entrance to the kitchen – was in my sights, and in my reach. The gleaming mahogany floors under my feet gave way to polished concrete – a risky, non-traditional choice, but one I would absolutely make again – as I stepped out of the ballroom, and quickly pushed my way through the double-doors.

Just beyond the stainless steel prep tables and appliances, through the pantry stacked high with higher-end ingredients used at the hotel restaurant, there was a door that led to the service elevator, which led to the parking deck, which led to my beloved red Jaguar. Once I got behind that wheel, I was *gone.*

I tread carefully in my heels, even though I'd insisted on slip-resistant flooring for all of the service areas. I dodged the head chef, avoided slamming into a tray-laden server, and waved at the lively line of dishwashers as I navigated through the kitchen, and into the quiet, unadorned hall that led to the service elevator.

I breathed a little sigh of relief as I pressed the button to bring the elevator down. That relief was short-lived, because my phone began buzzing against my chest from its tucked-in position in my bra.

I couldn't help a preemptive roll of my eyes as I pull the vibrating device from my dress. Before I looked at it, I glanced at the floor number display for the elevator. *Twelve more floors to go.* The impatient tap of my high-heeled foot against the tile echoed through the hall, and knowing that I shouldn't put it off, I turned my cell phone screen toward me so I could see the missed call.

*Shit.*

It was Braxton. And if *he* was looking for me, there was no doubt in my mind that his twin, Lincoln, was looking for me as well. A sudden thought occurred to me, and my eyes slid up the wall to the corner of the ceiling, where a security camera was mounted. My first inclination was to move and find a blind spot. But that was useless, because there were cameras in the elevator too.

Right on cue, the elevator chimed to let me know it had arrived, and the doors slid open to reveal that it was blissfully empty. I slipped inside and pushed the button that would take me to the parking deck. After that, I jabbed at the button to close the doors, and held my breath as the elevator began to move.

My phone buzzed again, and I was reasonably sure one or both of the twins knew I was in the elevator, but I didn't care. I turned my back on the doors I'd used to enter the elevator, and when it stopped at the executive level of the parking deck, the doors on the other side opened.

*Yes!*

My heels echoed on the pavement as I sped through the

rows of cars with purpose. I was congratulating myself on the wisdom of keeping a spare valet key in the little storage compartment built into the protective case I used on my phone. The screen lit up with another call, and I ignored that one too.

A big, joyous smile spread across my lips as I spotted Kitten, – my bright red jag – and I'd already pushed the key into the lock when a big hand came down to rest on my shoulder.

"Going somewhere, Mrs. Haley?"

*Shit. Shit. Shit.*

And now, here we were.

I was dumbfounded at first by Dex's presence, so he explained that he'd been brought on as my personal security – something I didn't even realize I needed. I knew without having to ask that Braxton was behind that. After all, I only knew Dexter because he was Brax & Lincoln's friend.

I'd demanded to be taken back into the party, where I'd downed several glasses of champagne. I may have gotten a tiny bit loud, ranting about trifling men and whores, before Braxton left his pretty little prey at the bar to cut me off, insisting that it was time for my night to end. I snatched one more glass from a passing waiter as Dex escorted me out.

Hence, him thinking I was drunk.

I *wasn't* drunk.

Maybe a little tipsy.

When he realized how he was holding me, and that my nipples were dangerously close to being pressed into his chest, he drew back.

"Let's get you into bed Mrs. Haley."

I grinned. "Dexter, are you deaf? That's *exactly* what I've been saying."

He sighed, then pulled me to the door. Instead of my

keycard, he used his own, releasing his hold on my arm just long enough to get us through the door.

As soon as we were inside, I went to my bedroom door, then turned to him with a smile. "I think I hear something in my room. Come and check, please. You know, since you're private security and all."

Dexter raised an eyebrow, seemingly unamused by my antics, but he strode forward, emanating power with each step toward me. I didn't move from in front of the door, pressing my back to it, looking up at him with mischief in my eyes as he reached past me.

"Excuse me."

I moved aside, just enough that he could get through the door if he squeezed past me. He easily nudged me aside to enter, and I closed and locked the door behind him.

I stuck close, getting in his way while he checked the closets and under the bed, looking every bit as dangerous as I knew he was.

"Thank you *so* much," I said, smiling. "I feel a little bit better, but I think I'd like you to stick close. I need to take a bath, and I want you right in the room with me. You can take the pullout in here, so you can be nearby while I sleep. I've just got a funny feeling about tonight."

"Mrs. Haley…"

I waved a hand in the air, batting away his words. "You've known me for more than fifteen years, Dexter. Call me Nash, like everybody else."

"*Nashira.*"

A chill ran up my spine at the way my name rolled off his lips. If he called himself *scolding* me, saying my full name, with authority, in that deep, sexy voice wasn't the direction he wanted to take.

"Yes?" I asked innocently, clasping my hands behind my back as I smiled.

He shook his head, but I caught a hint of a smile. "There's no one here. There is no threat to you. Waiting outside your door is more than sufficient."

"But I don't feel safe."

"You have no reason not to."

Pressure mounted between my eyes as my headache built in intensity, and I decided to go ahead and play my trump card. "You realize this isn't really up for debate, right? Your job is security, so… secure me."

"I was hoping I could appeal to logic here. Hoping that you would see reason."

I laughed quietly, almost under my breath, then reached under my arm to unhook my dress. Once that was undone, I grabbed the zipper, sliding it down and letting my dress fall away from my body. I stood in front of him, nothing covering my honey-toned skin except a thong.

"Dex… you *assume* I'm a reasonable person."

>>||<<

I flicked bubbles at Dex from my position in the bath tub, then laughed at the stern look he shot me from across the room. He was trying in his best to maintain a serious façade, and I was trying my best to break it. It was going to be interesting to see who won our little battle. But… with my particular goal, I didn't see how either of us *lost.*

Sinking deeper into the bubbles, I closed my eyes, imagining that he was kneeling next to the tub. Buried up to his elbows in the hot, soapy water, hands exploring my hot, soapy skin, his fingers working between my hot, soapy thighs. I put my own fingers there, slipping and sliding, letting out a low moan of satisfaction before I opened my eyes to find Dex staring right at me.

I grinned as I lowered my gaze to the conspicuous bulge straining the front of his pants, then snagged my bottom lip with my teeth as I pushed two fingers inside of me, releasing a little whimper of pleasure. "Would you like to join me Dex? It's always so much more fun with two."

That muscle in his jaw clenched again, and to my surprise, he actually moved closer, stopping right at the edge of the tub before he knelt down. I opened my legs, hooking one over the lip of the tub, causing steamy water to move over the edge, and drip from my dangling foot.

"Mrs. Haley... why are you playing this game with me?"

I chuckled. "I'm not playing."

"*Shit*, Nashira!" He jumped back – too late – as I sent a wave of water and soap bubbles at him, splashing him hard enough that he was definitely going to have to come out of that suit.

He snatched a towel from the warming cabinet beside the tub to wipe his face, then to my delight, removed his soaked jacket. While his back was turned, I slipped out of the tub, padding across the heated tile to approach him from behind. "Sorry Dex," I said, running a hand up his arm. He stiffened at my touch, then turned to face me.

The look on his face was in direct opposition to his body language, which was pushing me away. His *eyes*, on the other hand, were filled with a magnetic sort of lust that made my nipples hard as his gaze traveled over my soapy, naked body.

"*Fuck*." He muttered under his breath, and I resisted the urge to tell him "*yes, please*." He'd been the star of my private sexual fantasies for a long time, and I was more than ready to turn those desires into reality. "Can you cover up, please?"

He stalked over to the warmer and pulled a bath sheet

from one of the shelves, unfolding and wrapping it around me. I dropped it as soon as he let it go, but he was quick, and had it back around my body in no time, holding it in place himself.

"Why are you doing this?" he asked, hissing the words between his teeth. "You trying to get my ass kicked or something?"

"Don't be dramatic," I said, leaning into him, which elicited a groan.

"If one of the twins or Malcolm were to walk in here right now—"

"The only keycards that work for my suite are yours and mine. And besides, I would remind my brothers and stepfather that I'm a grown woman. As I'm reminding you that you're technically on *my* payroll, not theirs."

He narrowed his eyes. "What does that mean?"

"It means… maybe we can work out some different employment terms. A better compensation package?"

His scowl deepened, but then he shook his head and began to laugh. "Mrs. Haley… are you trying to pay me to have sex with you?"

"Please stop calling me Mrs. Haley like you didn't take me to my senior prom," I said, looking him right in the eyes as I snaked my hand between us. "I would *never* pay for sex, but I would make sure you were well-compensated for any undisclosed additional duties."

For a long moment, he said nothing, then shook his head again. "Mrs. Ha—*Nashira*. You're a beautiful woman. *Bad as hell.* Do you know how many bold muthafuckas lives' I'm going to have to threaten on a daily basis for trying to get close to you? If you have an itch you need scratched, why not—"

"'*If*' I have an itch?" I ran my hands over the bulge in the front of his pants, and we *both* groaned. "Your dick is hard, so

I know you want to do this. I need you to stop playing. *Give it to me.*"

"I'm not an escort. I don't fuck for pay."

I lifted an eyebrow, then squeezed his dick. "What then?"

He grinned. "Nothing," he said, bringing his face closer to mine. "What would your husband think?" he whispered against my mouth, so close that his lips brushed mine as they moved.

*Wait... so, he doesn't know?*

I mean… I was still wearing my rings. The family had done a masterful job – so far – of keeping my divorce quiet and out of the press, at least until we got past this grand opening. But I wondered why Dex didn't know?

I'd been honestly shocked to see him when he caught me in the parking garage, because he hadn't been around for years, and now here he was. And apparently… my brothers hadn't told him I was newly single. I didn't know what they were thinking, putting *him*, of all people, right in my space when I was in an emotional, vulnerable state, but the sight of him had filled me with a kind of manic energy. I'd spent a lot of tears and a lot of time trying to overcome an – obviously – unreciprocated schoolgirl crush that wouldn't seem to go away.

He was still good friends with my brothers, and every time his name would come up, it made my heart race. To thirteen-year-old me, seventeen-year-old Dexter had been the perfect forbidden crush. Tall, and quiet, and sexy, ignoring the hell out of me while they played basketball in the driveway.

He'd still been perfect when I was sixteen and he was twenty. The twins were home from college, he was home on military leave, and they'd gotten drunk and passed out in front of the TV in the basement. I snuck down there, and snuck into his arms, letting my hands explore his body over his clothes. But Dexter wasn't as inebriated as I thought. My hand was halfway in his sweats, seeking something I had no idea how to do anything with when he caught my wrist in his firm grip, then snatched me upward, over his mouth-watering muscled body, until we were face to face. My heart had soared, hoping that maybe he would kiss me, but he looked at me with narrowed eyes, then whispered for me to *"take my little ass back upstairs and don't try this shit again."*

When I was eighteen, and he was twenty-two, he was home on leave again. The twins were still off at college, senior year, so Dexter and Malcolm sat together in the front room of the house as I paced the floor, waiting for a prom date who never showed. I found out later that my date's father had passed away, but at the time, I was heartbroken, thinking I'd been stood up. So, in a move that was shocking only to me, Malcolm put Dexter in a tux, gave him the keys to one of his luxury cars, and told him to take me to my prom before I missed it.

My little teenaged heart was on fire, because *still*, for me, Dex was perfect. He danced with me, took the corny-ass prom pictures, made sure I was never thirsty, submitted to being fawned over by my friends. He made my prom a beautiful night. And then afterwards, when I quietly offered, then demanded, then begged him to take my virginity, he graciously declined.

It seemed like he was always ignoring me, pushing me away, refusing me, and I didn't like it. I understood now that the age difference had been a factor when we were younger, but what was the problem now?

I snatched the fat diamond ring set from my hand, and threw both pieces at him. He easily dodged the impact, then backed me against the hard marble counter. The smooth, cold surface was stimulating against my skin, and I couldn't think of anything except him propping me on top of the counter as he slammed into me.

"Dex, please?" I asked, tugging against the edges of the towel, trying to open it. "Is there something wrong with me? Am I ugly to you? Why not *me*?"

He frowned, keeping the towel pulled tight around my body. "What the fuc—Nashira, what the hell are you talking about?"

When I dared to meet his eyes, it was like they saw straight through me, right into the depths of my soul. Suddenly, the energy for my attempted seduction was gone, I was staunchly sober, and my alcohol-lowered inhibitions were back at full speed.

What the hell was I doing?

"Nothing," I whispered, dropping my gaze. I wrapped my arms around my body. "You can let go."

He didn't move. "Nash, tell me what's happening. Where were you going, when I caught you in the parking garage?"

"Nowhere, Dex. And if we could pretend this never happened, just like the other times?"

"Or you could tell me what's going on."

I sucked my teeth, casting my eyes away from him. "Yeah, like you really care."

The mood instantly shifted. Strong fingers wrapped around my jaw to turn my face back in his direction. "Why would you say that shit to me?"

"Because it's true," I spat back, smacking his hand away. "Or are you going to act like you *didn't* leave?"

"Are you going to act like you *didn't* get married?!"

I did my best to shove him away from me, but Dex's body was too solid. An impenetrable wall, unwilling to be moved, and I growled my frustration in his face. "I got married *because* you left!"

Tears pricked my eyes as I remembered the last time I'd

seen Dex before today. Six years ago, when I was twenty-two, and he was twenty-six. He'd been injured, badly, and had to come home from a tour overseas. I went to the military hospital with Lincoln and Braxton to see him, and somehow, we'd found ourselves alone in the room. I was still carrying that torch for Dexter, still wanted him so badly.

I'd laced my fingers with his, and leaned in close. Seeing him like this, in a hospital bed, added a sense of urgency to my plea. *"Let's just try it, and see what happens. I've caught how you look at me when you think nobody is looking. We're both grown now, Dex."*

But… he'd looked me right in the eyes, with certainty, and shook his head. *"Your brothers."*

And then their voices were on the other side of the door, and I snatched my hand from his and stepped away from the bed. I mumbled an excuse about the bathroom, then hurried away to cry my eyes out, because I'd been so sure that his reluctance had been about our age. And I didn't buy that it was about my brothers either, because while they were protective, they weren't overbearing about that kind of thing.

"I had to finish my responsibility with the military."

"And then you got out! But you didn't come back, did you? You got well, you accepted your honorable discharge, and then you got your ass on a plane to go to the other side of the planet. And I only know that because of the twins."

He groaned then, a low rumble that in spite of my anger, hit me right between the legs. "Nashira…"

"What? No *Mrs. Haley* anymore?"

"Don't be like this…"

I let out what was – admittedly – a shrill, crazy-sounding peal of laughter. "Don't be like this? Don't be like what, Dex? Don't be angry that you couldn't even pick up a phone and call? Not even hi, bye, kiss my ass, nothing?!"

"I called myself respecting your marriage!"

"*For what?*" I asked, attempting again to push him away. "It's not like Matt did, why should you?"

"Wait, *what?*" Dex grabbed my chin again, turning me to face him, and I didn't bother to resist. "What are you talking about?"

I shook my head, then pulled away from his touch. "Matt was cheating on me," I said, my voice cracking with unexpected emotion. "I found out yesterday, but it had been going on for years. Basically since we got married. He…" I stopped to let out a snort of laughter. "He gave *her* a gorgeous diamond necklace for their "anniversary". I got a text from him while he was in Vegas for ours. So my marriage didn't need or deserve your respect, because it's over."

"I had no idea. I'm sorry." Calloused hands gripped my arms, soothing me with a simple touch that I wanted to shake away. The compassion in his voice, and the raw, open regret in his eyes made the hollow ache that had built in my chest since yesterday ring even more sharply.

I shrugged – to get away from his touch, and to pretend I was unaffected. "Whatever. Can you move?"

That time, he obliged me, stepping back so I could leave the bathroom.

Tears pricked my eyes as I stepped back into the bedroom. I headed straight for the dresser, dropping my towel along the way as I snatched open the drawer that held my underwear.

Dex took a position near the door, his back against the wall, and I could see his face reflected in the mirror. As I pulled out a pair of panties, anger pricked my chest again.

"So, you were doing security while you were overseas too, right? This is your new, post-military career tract, huh? High end escorts, was it? You ever fuck one of them? I know they know all kinds of neat little tricks and—"

"*Stop.*"

"Why?" I shot back, turning to face him with my panties clutched in my hand. "Tell me something… do you still just see me as Braxton and Lincoln's little sister? Hmm? Is that all I am to you, why you'll never touch me? I don't measure up to other women?"

His eyes narrowed. "That is absolutely not the case."

"And that is absolutely *bullshit*," I snapped, jabbing a finger is his direction. "But whatever, Dex." I turned, then pulled my panties on before grabbing a tank top from a different drawer. "I should have known better. I *do* know better. You didn't give a shit about me, you were just humoring me because I was your friends' little sister. A Naïve ass teenager with a crush, so hungry for some attention that I actually thought you might have feelings for me."

I was completely aware of how ridiculous I probably looked, nearly naked and teary-eyed. I haphazardly pulled my tank top over my head, and got even more pissed off when I got tangled in it. I closed my eyes to snatch it off, and when I opened them again, Dex was right in front of me, his eyes burning with a soul-searing intensity that made a shiver run down my spine.

He looked me right in the eyes as he spoke, in a low voice that commanded obedience, "Don't *ever* doubt the way I felt about you."

"*Felt?*" I whispered that little one-worded question like I didn't want him to hear it, but I did. I needed that answer like I needed my next breath. He cupped my face in his hands, and his mouth crashed onto mine. He was kissing me. *Finally*, he was kissing me.

There was no slow seduction, no sweet pecks to build the tension, there was just Dex's tongue in my mouth, probing and tasting, devouring me like he was starving. I pushed myself up on my toes, draping my arms around his neck to pull myself closer as he tugged my lip between his teeth. My knees went weak, and molten heat built between my thighs as his tongue sank into my mouth again, stroking slow and deep until he took my breath away, and finally drew back.

"*Feel*, Nashira."

My fingers wrapped around his collar, tugging at it to keep him from moving away. "Then what's holding you back?"

His gaze snagged mine, and we stared at each other, until something in him shifted again. He grabbed me at the hips, pulling me up against his body and hooking his thumbs into the sides of my panties before he answered.

"Nothing that matters enough right now for me to let you keep these on."

>> ||| <<

I held my breath as Dex dragged my panties down over my legs, deliberate, unhurried. I didn't exhale until he was kneeling in front of me, not saying anything, just running a single fingertip up the inside of my thigh. It was a submissive position, him at my feet like I was royalty, but then he looked up, right into my eyes, and said simply, "Open". I spread my legs as wide as they could go.

There was no question about who was in charge.

His hands slid up the backs of my thighs, gripping and squeezing as he pulled me even closer. He buried his nose between my legs and inhaled deeply, letting out a low, bliss-filled groan. I gasped, gripping his shoulders for balance when I felt the warmth of his tongue on me, licking and teasing the insides of my thighs just before he covered me with his mouth.

"De-*ahhh, shhhhiiiittt.*" I couldn't even catch a breath enough to speak intelligible words, so I bit down on my lip, squeezing my eyes shut instead. His hands were on my ass, kneading and gripping and pulling me closer to his mouth. His tongue moved, lapping at me like he was thirsty, drinking me in, devouring me, making me go weak in the knees.

"*Ahhhh.*" I couldn't close my mouth. Every time I tried, his tongue dipped a little deeper, circled my clit a little faster, harder. I moaned, whimpered, as tears of pleasure pricked my eyes, and then – holy hell – he plunged his fingers into me. I dug my nails into his shoulders, involuntarily rising onto my toes as he pushed deeper, swirling and moving like he was searching for a particular spot, and then – sweet Jesus – he found it.

"St-stop. Stop, stop, stop," I begged, trying to push his head back, trying to get away from him.

He looked up, his mouth still on me, eyes glittering with mischief as he shook his head. He flattened his tongue, giving me a deliciously long, slow lick before he pulled away. "This is what you wanted, right?" He spread me open with his fingers, then kissed me there, making my knees buckle a little. "You offered this to me, and I'm accepting. You don't get to hold back. You're gonna give me all of you, everything. You understand?" He sucked my clit into his mouth, gently teasing with his teeth and tongue until I whimpered out a "yes".

"Then stop playing," he said, looking me right in the eyes as he pushed his fingers in me again. "And let me make you come for me."

"O-*okaaaaaaa—ahhh!*" I shamelessly bucked against his mouth as he buried his face between my legs, consuming me with wide, flat licks, and circles around my clit, filling me with deep, plunging strokes of his fingers.

Then I was tingling. All over, everywhere, and my legs were trembling so hard I could barely stay up. I closed my eyes, opened my mouth and cried out as the pressure at my core imploded and I came, with my fingers pressed into Dexter's skull, holding him in place.

As I came down from my orgasm, he kissed me everywhere, moving over my thighs, up to the tiny silver ring in my belly button. He pulled us backward until he was seated on the bed, with me standing in front of him, then moved up to my breasts, where he sucked my nipples into hard, sensitive peaks.

"I need to be inside you. Right now."

*Needed?*

He eased me backwards enough that he could stand up, and started to unbutton his shirt, still wet from me splashing him in the bath. I moved his hands aside, pulling my lip between my teeth as I took over. Dex lifted an eyebrow, smirking as I stripped him out of his shirt, then dropped my hands to his belt. He toed off his shoes, then stood still as I unbelted his pants. He drew in a deep breath as I slid my fingers in the waistband of his boxers and took his dick in my hands, running my thumb over the smooth tip.

I tugged his boxers down, and he kicked them off, then allowed me to push him back on the bed. I climbed on top of him, and when our eyes met, his expression made my breath catch in my throat. Either I was imagining it, or he was just as amazed as I was that we were finally, *finally* doing this.

He reached up, cupping my face in his hand to pull me into a kiss. His fingers dug into my short-cropped natural curls, grazing my scalp as he invaded my mouth with his tongue. I maneuvered my hands between us to touch his erection, then moved my fingers over him in firm, unhurried strokes.

"Nashira…"

*Mmmm.* Why did my name have to sound so good on his lips?

"Yeah, Dex?" I mumbled, without opening my eyes.

"About… protection."

Oh.

I opened my eyes then. "What about it?"

"I really just want to feel *you.* Nothing between us. But, I'll understand if—"

"I'm okay with that. I'm on birth control, and me and Matt…" I trailed off, then shook my head. "Not for a while. And I trust you."

A little part of me hated that was true, after he'd dodged me all these years, but Dexter was one of the few people I trust implicitly. Maybe *because* he'd been so protective, even shielding me from *him.* He'd cared for and guarded me differently, but almost just as much as my brothers had. Dexter had threatened boys, changed tires, let me cry on his shoulder, picked me up in the middle of the night without asking questions. If he wanted to do this without protection, there wasn't a doubt in my mind that it was safe for me.

And… I wanted to feel him with nothing between us too.

Dex kissed me slow and deep, moving his hands to my breasts to cup and squeeze, then down to my hips to guide me onto him. He swallowed my moan as he sank into me, burying himself as deep as he could go, and neither of us moved. I'd closed my eyes as he filled me up, and now I was just… enjoying the feeling of him inside me.

Finally.

I kissed him back, rolling my hips against as I began to move. I pressed my hands against his shoulders, sitting up, using the leverage of my knees against the bed to grind onto him deeper. But then… he sat up too. Wrapped me in his arms, holding me close as I rode him. I draped my arms over his shoulders, pressed my hands to the back of his neck, keeping him against me as he dropped his mouth to my breasts again.

Making love, to Dex, was *everything* I'd imagined. He felt incredible inside me, stretching me with deep strokes as he rocked into me, meeting me with a stroke to match my every rise and fall. He flipped me onto my back, wrapping my legs around his waist as he plunged, slow and deep. His mouth and tongue moved over my breasts, my neck, my jaw, my lips, any place he could reach. And his hands... his hands were everywhere. Touching, caressing my skin. He pulled back, propping my legs on his shoulders, kissing my toes as he pushed his hand between my legs.

He pressed his thumb to my clit, moving it in tight, fast circles, and I came unglued under him. Legs shaking, chest heaving, throbbing between my legs as he stroked harder, faster, harder, deeper, harder, faster until an orgasm crashed over me. He dropped my legs, wrapping his arms around me again to hold me close, burying his face in my neck as he plunged into me one last time. My eyes were shut tight, and I kept them that way, focusing on the sensation of my body milking him as he released.

When we could both move again, and breathe, Dex picked me up, carrying me into the shower. He soaped my body, washed me clean, and then I returned the favor before he carried me back to the bed. Neither of us said anything as we climbed under the covers. I snuggled close, and he let me, wrapping an arm around my waist as I settled against his chest and closed my eyes.

*Finally.*

>> ||| <<

"So... is it important now?"

Dex had his eyes closed, but opened them when I asked that question. We were still in bed, had been all morning, and had no plans to do anything else. Not as far as *I* was concerned.

"What are you talking about?" he asked, stroking a hand over my back as he shifted to see me better. I was draped over his chest, and I tipped my head up, propping my chin on his pecs.

"Last night... I asked you what was holding you back. You said it wasn't important enough to keep you from helping me out of my panties right then."

Dex chuckled. "I didn't say that."

"But that was the gist of it." I said, running my fingers over his abs. "And what I want to know now is... whatever was holding you back... what does it mean for us? Is this something that was just for tonight, or are we *doing* this?"

Letting out a heavy sigh, Dexter pulled me close, then planted a kiss on my forehead. "Nashira... you've always been beautiful to me. At first, yeah... you were my friend's little sister. But you have to understand, that I was already shocked that your brothers wanted to be friends with me anyway. I was the kid in busted sneakers and faded shirts. Y'all were like royalty."

"Because of my stepdad," I explained. "After our dad died, when it was just us and our mom? We didn't have anything, Dex. And then Malcolm came along and swept her off her feet, not caring that she had three kids that weren't his. His generosity, even after my mother refused to have us take his name so we could keep our biological father's memory... it's the only reason we lived like that."

Dexter shrugged. "I was a kid. I didn't know that at the time, I just knew your family had money, and mine didn't.

That's why your brothers went to college, and I went to the military. I had to provide. But… anyway, I definitely noticed you, Nashira. But you were untouchable for me. Family treasure, not to be disturbed, and I didn't want to mess up my friendship over you, when back then… I would have broken your heart."

"But what about when you got hurt?" I asked, running my tongue over my lips. "I reached out for you, and you basically pushed me away. We were grown, Dex."

"Yeah, we were. Grown, and mature enough to understand that I wasn't the kind of man that would satisfy you anywhere except in the bedroom. I'm not a business man, I don't drink Voss, I can't tell you the difference certain wines. I don't rub elbows with politicians, or drive a foreign car."

I sucked my teeth. "That's not what I *want*."

"That's exactly what you married, Nashira! Look at Matt!"

"*Screw* Matt," I said, sitting up. "I went with what I thought was safe, what everybody told me was a good match. And look at what happened. I don't want that again. I want somebody that makes my heart flutter, and makes me angry, and makes me fight for him. I want you, Dex."

He pushed out another heavy sigh, then swiped a hand over his face. "My line of work… I get *dirty*, sweetheart. It's not pretty. I'm *not* one of these pretty boys I've seen you date over the years."

"I don't expect you to be," I said, positioning myself so that I was straddling him, then brought my hands up to his chin. "The only thing I expect, if we do this, is for you not to break my heart."

"That's an empty guarantee."

I smiled. "I know. Do it anyway."

He shook his head, but the corners of his mouth teased a smile. "If we – no, *when* – no, *since* we're doing this…. I promise not to break your heart."

He reached for my hips, moving me backwards toward his dick.

I swatted his hands, then leaned down to kiss him again. "Now see… that was the easy part, wasn't it?"

"Easy part?" he murmured against my lips. "What's the hard part?"

"Convincing my brothers not to break your legs."

# BRAXTON & EDEN

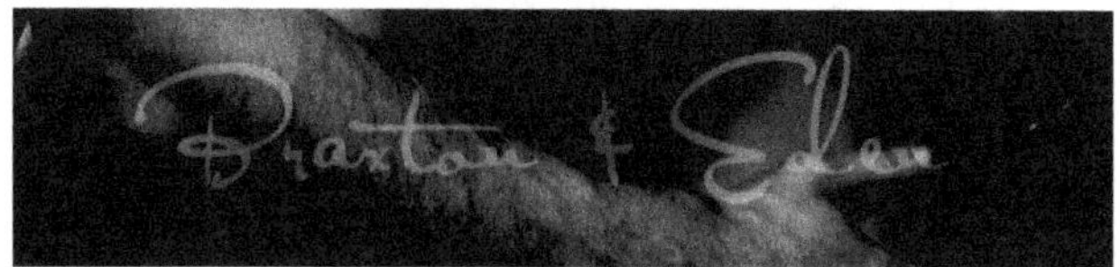

 could feel him watching me, long before he actually approached.

When I accepted a glass of champagne, when I stopped to admire the architecture, while I stood right in front of the live jazz band, letting my hips sway to the music, his eyes were on me. He didn't know it yet, but that was by design.

For a change, *he* wasn't the focus of the night. This event belonged to his sister, Nashira, and their stepfather, Malcolm Armstrong. The family patriarch had just finished the renovations to this, his twenty-second luxury hotel, and Nashira, who had a talent for event planning, had been the one to put this shindig together.

He was different tonight. It was strange, to find yourself so in tune with someone you'd never met that you could feed off their energy, reading their mood even when outwardly, the picture they presented was the same as usual.

To this crowd, many of them too lost in the ooh-ing and ah-ing over the extravagance of the hotel and the party, gossiping about the Drake/Armstrong family, and too busy sucking back drinks to offer anything more than surface-level attention to anyone around them, he was his normal self. In a room full of people who were mostly too rich to be useful, the tightness of his jaw went unnoticed. The tension in his shoulders didn't garner a second look, the frostiness in his gaze was dismissed as intoxication, and nobody was looking at his hands long enough for his clenched fists to seem out of place.

With a face and body like that, why the hell would anybody look at his *hands?*

Braxton Drake looked, as he always did, like luxury.

Impossibly smooth red-brown skin, impossibly fresh haircut, impeccably tailored gray suit, covering an exquisitely fit body. Everything about Braxton gave off a sense of shiny and new. Even his face was shaped to perfection, sharply cut angles in the right places, soft edges where he needed them, dusted with immaculately groomed facial hair. All qualities that could easily lend themselves to a pretty boy image, but no… Braxton wasn't pretty at all.

Mesmerizing… now *that* was a word that worked for him.

Magnetically warm brown eyes, a chiseled jaw, and a perfect sort-of-crooked smile certainly didn't hurt his appeal, but the most alluring thing about Braxton wasn't the way he looked. It was the way he walked.

Braxton stepped into a room like he owned it, shoulders squared, head high. He moved with a relaxed, confident stride, effortlessly navigating throngs of people who wanted his attention. He was a man of easy smiles, polished charm, and casual flirtations, the kind of man who could enter an area and before more than a few minutes passed, have a different woman hanging on either arm.

But *not* tonight.

Tight jaw, clenched fists, tense shoulders, cold eyes… something, someone, somewhere, was bothering Braxton, and I had a good feeling it was the marital drama involving his sister. Tonight was the kind of night he would be looking for a release, wanting an escape. I bit the inside of my lip to suppress a smile.

I was willing to be that distraction.

He chose the opening right next to me when he approached the bar, and ordered a Jack and coke. I glanced in his direction, admiring the view of his profile. When his eyes slid toward me, I quickly looked away, staring at the crushed ice lining the bottom of my own finished drink.

His gaze stayed with me while he waited, but I didn't look in his direction. "You're far too beautiful to be sitting here with an empty glass."

I kept my eyes down, pretending I didn't know he was talking to me. It was hard though, when my body reacted to the rich warmth of his voice like I was cold, and he was suddenly blanketing me in heat. I visibly shivered, and without looking, I knew he was smiling as he took the empty seat beside me at the bar. My heart started racing. I was only supposed to be *getting* his attention – not *enjoying* it.

"Am I supposed to believe you're shy?" he asked, not taking his eyes away from me as he accepted his drink. I knew this without looking up because his gaze was still locked on me, hot enough to burn my clothes right off my body. His demeanor had shifted, and the usual Braxton Drake was back. Smiling, charming, flirtatious, sexy… dangerous.

The answer to his question was *yes*, but that wasn't something he needed to know. I shook my head, then swallowed hard as I chanced a glance in his direction and my eyes caught, then held, his. "No," I said, my voice soft, barely audible over the loud jazz filling the ballroom. "I'm not shy, it's just… well, you're…" I let the sentence trail off. He didn't need me to tell him who he was, it was drilled into him all day, every day, Braxton Drake. Black royalty.

"You know who I am?"

I lifted an eyebrow, let out a nervous laugh. "Doesn't everybody?"

That may or may not have been the right answer, because almost immediately, his frosty wall went right back up. He shook his head, his eyes cold and bitter and he took a long swig from his drink. "They think they do."

"Think?" I asked, breaking eye contact as I pushed a handful of thick, wavy hair over my shoulder. "You're giving these people a lot of credit here, assuming they *think* at all."

Braxton chuckled, and I silently relished the sound as it set off little prickles of excitement over my bare skin. When I looked at him again, his lips were curved up at the edges, offering me just a hint of a smile. Something across the room caught his attention, and I followed his gaze to his gorgeous sister.

Nashira Haley – her married name – had no reputation for bad behavior. As a matter of fact, under different circumstances, she could have been a friend. Polished, poised, and about her business. Well... usually. Right now, she was swaying on her feet, and saying something I couldn't hear over the music, but the tall-and-sexy next to her didn't look amused. He touched her, trying to calm her, and I caught a glimpse of a gun at his waist.

*Oh... private security.*

Braxton let out a heavy sigh, then said, "I have to go, but... you have a good night."

And then he left my side, disappearing into the crowd of black glitterati.

I wanted to leave, badly. But I made myself sit there for another thirty minutes before I stood. Although the time was creeping closer to midnight, the party was in full swing. But, I wasn't there for the part anyway. The ornately carved glass of the doors that led to the foyer where flanked on either side by beefy security guards. The same guards had been there when I came in, so I paid them no mind as I approached, heading straight for the heavy iron handle.

"I need you to come with me, ma'am," one of them said to me. My breath caught in my throat as a hand came down on my wrist, then pulled me away from the door. There was no room to protest, no room to breathe, no room to even *see* who was guiding me around the edge of the swarm of people, through a side door, and into a small meeting room.

There was a table in the middle, surrounded by six chairs, and I was thrust – not roughly – into one. Before I could turn around, my abductor was gone, leaving me alone in the modernly-styled meeting room. I stood up, intending to try the door, when it was suddenly pulled open and Braxton stepped inside.

I took a step back. In this smaller space, with no one around except us, Braxton's presence assaulted my senses. My nostrils filled with the clean scent of his cologne, nipples hardened in reaction to the heat from his body. He seemed bigger somehow, and my mouth watered at the way his shirt stretched across his chest as he pushed his hands into his pockets.

"You're leaving already?" he asked, as he sat down at the edge of the table, his gaze landing on different parts of my body, lingering just long enough to grow hot under his attention.

I shrugged. "It's getting late. Have to sleep at some point, right? Why do you care if I'm leaving? You don't even know me."

"I know I want you to come upstairs and see my suite before you go."

My eyebrow twitched as I met his gaze with narrowed eyes. "Excuse me?"

"You heard what I said."

I propped a hand on my hip. "Do you think I'm some sort of Drake family groupie or something? Because I guarantee you, I'm—"

"Not at all. What makes you think you need to clarify what you are and aren't for me?"

"The fact that you feel comfortable asking me to come up to your room, when you don't even know my name." I crossed my arms, then glanced down, blushing when I saw how my action had lifted my breasts to attention in the tastefully skimpy summer blue dress I'd chosen for the night. I didn't drop them though, because *he* didn't need to know I regretted it. I scowled right into his gorgeous face.

He smirked. "I didn't ask you anything, Eden. I stated a desire."

The sound of my name rolling off his lips in that deep, rumbling voice had dual effects on me. It was a little unnerving, because I hadn't shared that information with him. It was intriguing, for the same reason. Still, I took a step back.

"How do you know my name?"

"Isn't *why* do I know your name a more appropriate question?" He closed the distance between us, standing near enough to almost touch, invading my personal space. "I didn't want not knowing your name to be a reason for you to not oblige my request."

"So it *was* a request?"

His mouth twitched then, spreading into a smile that put his beautiful teeth on full display, but he ignored my question. "What would it take?"

"What would *what* take?"

"For you to say *'Yes, Mr. Drake. I'll come to your suite and let you... show me around.'* What conditions would have to be met?"

"*Mr. Drake?*" I arched an eyebrow.

He pulled his bottom lip between his teeth, suppressing a

laugh, and the image of his lip between *my* teeth flashed in my mind. Would his lips taste like Jack and coke? "I wouldn't make you call me Mr. Drake."

"Make me?"

"Do you realize you're responding to everything I say with a question?"

I gave him my sweetest smile as I looked up to meet his eyes. "How do you know my name?"

Braxton drew in a deep breath through his nose, then lifted his hand to my face as he pushed the air back out. I kept my eyes locked with his as he brushed his thumb along my jaw, then swept a hand through my hair.

"The bartender carded you, Eden Frazier, twenty-eight years old. What would it take to get you to come up and get a tour of my suite?"

"I'm not a whore."

"Never said you were. Give me an answer."

I shifted on my platform heels as I looked up, meeting his eyes again as his hands went to my waist. "What if the answer is no?"

Braxton took a deep breath, and his teeth scraped across his lip again. "Then my feelings will be hurt, and I'll have to step aside and let you walk out of here."

"And...," I murmured, moving forward the half inch it took to just barely press my body against his. "What if the answer is... *yes?*"

His hands moved down, gripping my ass, squeezing as he pulled me tighter against him. "If the answer is yes... then what are we waiting for?"

>> ||| <<

*M*y mother raised me better than to sleep with a stranger.

Well… actually my mother didn't raise me, but that's outside of the point.

If I had a mother who'd raised me not to sleep with strangers, I *still* would have left the hotel's grand opening with Braxton, knowing what his intentions were, because sometimes a girl just does was she has to. And this was something I had to do.

My dress, my hair, my jewelry, my demeanor, hell, even the fragrance I wore, were all chosen to appeal specifically to *his* senses. It was all a carefully curated seduction, to make sure I ended up in his room.

He led me through the kitchen, to a service elevator that had to come all the way down from the 60th floor. He was occupied on his phone while we waited, and as I watched him, I wondered what he was like in bed. If you believed those erotic romance novels, he would blow my mind, because every millionaire did. He would smack it, flip it, rub it down, and then chain me to the bedposts and pleasure me until I came 36 times, and only then would he pull his dick out.

Yeah, right.

More likely? He would blanch, get flustered, and act like I was being completely unreasonable if I insisted he put his face between my legs. He would pump a lame excuse for a dick into me maybe ten times before he exploded, then explain that I was too hot for him to last very long. I would get my ass out of there, and shower at home, lest he get any ideas about joining me to subject me to another round of wack sex. Braxton was rich, smart, and fine as hell. His bedroom skills had to suck. It was science. A man couldn't have *everything* going for him.

If I *had* to sleep with him… well, it would be a small price to pay, if it got me to my desired result. Besides, I'd willingly dated and slept with much worse men than Braxton.

The elevator chimed to let us know it had arrived, and Braxton gestured for me to enter first. I did, using the mirrored walls for a quick check of my appearance as he stepped in behind me, then pressed the button that would take us up – *way* up – to his floor.

I'd worn my hair in its natural state of thick, wavy curls. I'd taken special care after my shower, to make sure my deep mahogany skin glowed against the rich blue of my flirty cocktail dress. My heels were high, jewelry minimal, and anywhere Braxton happened to put his nose would smell like paradise. I had condoms in the tiny clutch purse in my hand. I was prepared for everything except the hot, lusty feeling that swept over my body when he looked at me.

Our eyes met in the mirror as he turned to me, and the elevator doors closed behind him. The heat of his body made me squirm a little as he approached, and then in a move I wasn't expecting… he pushed me against the wall. Not a shove, and not violent, just… a *push*, before he invaded my senses, destroying any semblance of personal space.

"You are… beyond beautiful," he said, running a hand over the side of my body, letting it rest against my hip. I shivered against the cold mirror as he pressed against me from behind, and quickly realized that Braxton didn't have an "excuse" for a dick. If I felt what I thought I was feeling, growing harder against my back, he had plenty of it. Enough to spread around.

"Are you okay?" he asked, leaning over my shoulder as his fingers playing with the hem of my dress. "You shivered. Are you having second thoughts?"

I swallowed hard.

*Yes.*

"No."

My breath caught in my throat as he swept my hair to the side, then pressed his lips to my neck. His mouth was deliciously hot, and he was generous with it, kissing and sucking and biting until I arched against him, pressing my ass against that bulge in his pants, letting out a moan that I tried and failed to hold in.

Braxton groaned against my neck. "So goddamned *sexy*," he murmured, then sucked my neck hard, enough to leave a mark I'd be pissed about tomorrow. Tonight, it just felt good.

One of his hands was pressed against the mirror beside my head. The other moved under my dress, gripping my thigh to ease my legs apart. I moaned again as he touched me, skimming my thighs, tracing the waistband of my underwear as he kissed my neck. *Teasing* me, until finally, he swept a finger from my opening to my clit, then trailed it back and forth through my panties.

This wasn't supposed to feel this good. I was supposed to be alert, focused, keeping a clear head while I accomplished my agenda. Instead, I was panting, eyes squeezed tight, rocking my body against his hand, damn near on the verge of begging him to put his fingers in me. I whimpered as he pressed his thumb to my clit, and he nipped my shoulder, soothing the slight sting with a kiss.

I pulled my lip between my teeth, trying to suppress another moan, but he moved his hand from the wall, using his thumb to urge me to open my mouth. "Don't be quiet on me," he muttered against my ear, then slid his fingers under the damp lace of my panties. "Be vocal. Moan, scream, whatever you're feeling. I want to hear you."

And then the elevator chimed, letting us know we'd made it to his floor.

I hated myself a little for feeling a sense of loss when he moved his hand from between my legs. He grabbed my hand

and led me out of the elevator, down a short hallway, and into his suite.

"This is me," he said, his voice completely casual, like he hadn't been an inch away from fingering me in the elevator. He pressed me against the wall beside the door, towering over me, invading my space again with his scent of citrus and leather. "You still want that tour?" he asked, standing so close that I could feel his dick against my stomach.

From somewhere, I found enough composure to do a little seduction of my own, biting my lip as I rested my head on the wall, staring up at him with innocent eyes. "I thought that's what I was coming up here for."

He smirked, then shook his head. "You came up here because you want me to fuck you."

"Do I?"

I gasped as his fingers went between my legs again, searching and probing until they were under my panties, then inside of me. "As wet as you are," he said, dipping his head to kiss me as he moved his hand, plunging into me with slow, deep strokes. "You definitely, *definitely* do."

>>|||<<

From the moment our lips touched, I knew I was in over my head. Braxton didn't kiss me like this was some cheap one night stand. Hell, he could have just not kissed me at all. Instead, he took my mouth in measured, intoxicating licks that tasted like whiskey. His fingers between my legs fell into a sweet, tortuous cadence with his tongue in my mouth. Flicking, teasing, making delectably wet noises before he sank in deep.

The part of my mind that remained lucid wondered what the fuck I was doing. Why was I here, letting a man who was a virtual stranger, a man I should *hate* for the things he'd done, inside of my body, letting him learn what buttons to press to turn me on? Why *this* course of action, that required me to taste him, and opened the door for me to get hooked on the feeling of his tongue in my mouth?

Braxton dropped his lips to my neck, bathing my skin in kisses from shoulder to collarbone, then back up my neck until he reached my ear. "I can't decide if I want to taste you first, or if I want to be inside you," he murmured, then tugged my earlobe between his teeth. "What should I do, Eden?" he asked, then plunged his fingers deeper, taking my breath away, making it impossible for me to actually answer.

I whimpered my disappointment when he pulled away his hand. My eyes fluttered open in time to catch his smirk before he licked me off his fingers, then kissed me, sweeping my mouth with his tongue.

"It's an impossible choice, isn't it?" he asked, sucking my bottom lip as his fingers found their way back between my legs. He pressed his thumb to my clit and then plunged inside, pumping his hand harder, faster, with purpose. "Eden… That means paradise, right? Do I want to taste paradise, or feel it around my dick?"

And just like that, he was in my head, making me rethink my entire plan. His tongue was in my mouth, swallowing my cries of pleasure. His fingers were inside me, making my legs shake, taking away my ability to think clearly. He was in me, everywhere, in harmony.

Shit.

"Eat you or fuck you, beautiful?" he asked, kissing my ear. He had me pushed up on the wall, feet nowhere near the ground as he stroked me with his hand. "Answer me."

"I—*ahhhhhhh!*" As soon as I opened my mouth, he

increased the pressure of his thumb on my clit, and my mind blanked in response.

"Answer the question. Eat you or fuck you?"

Pressure coiled in me, fast. I tried to speak, but my breath came in short pants, words came out as frantic moans.

*"Eat you or fuck you,"* he asked, again and again as I rocked against his hand. He growled it in my ear, like he didn't understand that I couldn't answer while he drove my body like this.

"Answer me," he demanded, using the hand that wasn't between my legs to grab my chin between his forefinger and thumb. The other fingers pressed against my throat, making it hard to swallow, or even breathe, but Braxton leaned closer, snaring my gaze, forcing me to lock eyes with him. "Tell me what you want, Eden. *Now.* Taste you or fuck you?"

I whimpered against his mouth as he leaned in to kiss me, increasing the pressure on my throat and my clit at the same time. I felt dizzy, and high, and so damned good I could scream. Hot, electric tingles erupted all over my skin, and when he pressed his forehead to mine, commanding me again to answer his question, I belted out words I'd never in my life said to anyone else.

"Fuck me, *please.*"

The 'please' was barely off my lips before Braxton's tongue was in my mouth, licking and sucking and devouring the sound that wrenched its way from the depths of my throat as I came.

*Hard.*

So hard that I didn't remember moving from the wall by his front door, into the kitchen. I was still fuzzy when he took my forgotten purse from my hand where it'd been clutched the whole time, tossing it onto the counter. He unzipped my dress, letting it drop to the floor, then stripped the delicate panties away from my legs.

Standing behind me, he slid his hands up my thighs, over my stomach, up to my breasts. He groaned against the back of my neck as he cupped and squeezed, then pinched and rolled my nipples between his fingers until I was panting again.

"Go bend over the counter," He whispered into my skin. "And leave your shoes on."

I nodded my agreement, then did as he said, listening to the distinct sounds of him undressing himself. It was... soothing, somehow. The thump of his shoes hitting the floor, the soft swish of fabric falling together, the quiet rip of a foil package, the subtle pad of his bare feet on the tile as he came closer, standing right behind me.

I let out a quiet gasp when he touched me. His hands were hot and inquisitive, touching me everywhere. My thighs, between my legs, gripping my ass cheeks and spreading me apart. My skin grew heated under his gaze, waiting for him to touch me again, and then I felt him. His nose was practically *in* me, he'd buried his face so deep, and he covered my clit with his mouth and sucked.

I nearly came right off the counter.

He pressed a hand to my back, keeping me still as he gave me a long, hungry, exhilarating lick from my clit to the small of my back, and then he grabbed my shoulders, plunging inside of me. My hands searched for something to grip, but my fingers slipped and slid over the smooth granite surface of the island as he pulled me back.

His hands slid down my arms to grip the edge of the counter, and I balanced myself against his solid frame. In my heels, I was at the perfect height for his strokes as he slammed into me, again and again, groaning against my ear. "Don't you dare hold back on me," he growled.

So I didn't.

Every moan, gasp, whimper, I let it out. I opened my

mouth wide as I rocked my hips back against him, meeting him stroke for stroke until he pushed me down over the counter again, and then propped my leg up beside me.

Then, I *screamed.* It was so, so, *so* good that I couldn't have stayed quiet if I wanted to. I cried out his praises, a chorus of *yes, yes, yes, YES,* over and over until my throat was raw, and tears streamed down my face. My nipples were hard as rocks, and sensitive as they moved over the cold surface of the counter, adding yet another sensation to what was already sensory overload.

He was so, so deep, and his dick was so, so good, stretching me, filling me up, making my body weep with pleasure. He maneuvered his hand under me to brush his thumb against my clit, and that was all it took for me to come undone.

*"Ahhhh!"* My cry as I came was somewhere between a growl and a scream, and it echoed through the room as Braxton pulled me up. His hands were rough as he cupped my breasts, squeezing hard as he pumped into me with mind-numbingly deep strokes. And then... somehow I was coming again, or maybe I'd never stopped, but bliss washed over me in waves, making me light-headed and dizzy, making me tingle all over.

I erupted in spasms, clenching around him as Braxton slammed into me one more time, with my body pulled tight against his. My legs went weak, but his arms were around me, keeping me up as I burst into tears.

My mind was so soaked in ecstasy that I wasn't embarrassed at first, but then it edged its way in. Braxton pulled out of me, and for a second I thought he was about to shove my dress at me and send me on my way, but then he turned me around and pulled me against him as I sobbed. And I... closed my eyes and buried my face in his neck, snuggling into the warmth of his arms.

I wasn't just in over my head.

I was *drowning.*

"You okay?" he asked, planting a kiss in my hair, then on my forehead, then easing me back so he could kiss me on the lips. "That was… intense."

I swallowed hard, then nodded. "Yes. I'm okay. And… yes. It was."

Our eyes met, and there was something, a certain vulner-ability in his that let me know – what had just passed between us was unexpected. Hell, he looked as baffled as I felt, but he was still hard against my stomach as his hands dropped lower, caressing my ass and hips.

"Let me go deal with this condom," he said, but I felt his reluctance to let me go. The way he moved back, keeping his hands on me until the very last second, then finally letting his fingertips drop, made something stir in my chest.

It wasn't until he was out of the room, and I turned back toward the counter where my eyes landed on my purse that I remembered why I was there.

*Shit.*

I moved quickly to the tiny bar that sat at the edge of his kitchen, pulling out two glasses and filling them with ice. I slipped my hand into my purse to remove a tiny vial and dripped the liquid into one of the glasses, replacing it before I went back to the bar. I scanned the bottles lining the bar, then chose a bottle of Hennessey. I'd just put the top back when I felt, rather than heard Braxton behind me.

How long had he been there?

I turned to face him, hoping that I didn't look *too* guilty standing there in front of the bar. But he smiled at me, then reached for my hand. "If you're not in a hurry to leave, I started the shower. I figured we could—"

"Yes," I said, my voice eager as I smiled back. "And, I took the liberty of fixing us some drinks." I turned around and grabbed the glasses, being careful about which one I put in his hand. I lifted mine to my lips and swallowed, counting on him to mimic my action.

I kept my face neutral when he raised his glass, finishing it in one gulp.

He put both glasses down on the counter, then swept me off of my feet, into his arms. He took off my shoes, tossing them somewhere in the vicinity of our clothes, then carried me into the suite's large, luxurious bathroom.

In the shower, he put me under the spray, then used a soft towel to soap and wash my skin before he made a comment about having paradise on his tongue. He sat down on the built in seat in the shower, then pulled me in front him. He draped my leg over his shoulder, then devoured me. He was messy with it, noisy, slurping and sucking probing me with his fingers and tongue until I came again, and then he produced a condom from the shelf that held his shower products, and pulled me on top of him.

I wanted to rush through it. Make him come, get it over with, but my body wouldn't let me. He felt too good. I rode him in unhurried, languid strokes with his hands gripping my hips, caressing my breasts, holding my face while he kissed me like we were in love.

Afterwards, he carried me to his bed, where he pulled me close. His eyes were low, his movements sluggish, and as he drifted off, he mumbled something about never letting women sleep in his bed.

Guilt hit me then, but I brushed it off.

When his soft snores began to filter through the bedroom, I climbed out of the bed.

>> ||| <<

"*D*id you cut the cameras yet?" I spoke into my phone as pulled my useless panties back over my legs.

"Duh," came the sarcastic reply from Willow. "I've had control of the cameras since you and lover-boy got on the elevator. Which, by the way, that was hot as hell. I'm worried for you."

"Worried for me?" I asked, then pulled my dress back on and grabbed my purse. "Worried for me why?"

"E, that man just fucked your soul out of your body. You should be worried too."

I rolled my eyes as I headed for the little nook that served as Braxton's office, then took the flash drive out of my purse. "You watched us?"

"Hell yes. And I made a copy for you. We could sell this and make some money."

"We're not selling a sex tape, Willow."

"Hater."

I chuckled softly, then sat down in front of the computer. "Whatever. You just make sure you scrub me fixing those drinks and touching his computer off the tapes, okay?"

"You know I've got you. You ready?"

I nodded, knowing she could see me. "Tell me what to do."

>> ||| <<

"*Y*ou left without saying anything. Should I take that as a hint? – B. Drake"

Never mind that I hadn't actually given him my number. The sight of that text lighting the screen of my phone that morning after my little adventure with Braxton had made my heart race. Nearly a week had passed now, and instead of deleting it, I kept going back, running my fingers over the words.

I was off-kilter.

Braxton had thrown my balance out of whack.

Never, *ever* had a one night stand remained so clearly at the front of my mind. Hell, no sexual experience *period* played so vividly in my head as my time with Braxton. I never knew when it would hit me. The memories of him inside me made my knees week, the memory of his fingers on my skin made it impossible to think, and the feeling of his mouth on me was implanted so deep I doubted I could ever forget.

And that was a problem. All of it was a problem for which I had no solution that made viable sense. Maybe I could just text him back, sleep with him again, but that would have just further complicated things.

Things like this meeting.

Nervous energy made me fidget in my seat. I played with the binding of the folio in my hands, tugged at the hem of my skirt, counted the floor tiles. Anything to occupy my time enough not to read that text again, daydreaming about things that could never be. Anything to keep me from vomiting in response to the massive knot of anxiety that had been building in my stomach since I woke up.

"Ms. Frazier?" My head popped up, and I swallowed hard as I gave the smiling receptionist my attention.

"Yes?"

"They'll see you now."

I smiled back, nodded, and somehow convinced my legs to raise me from my seat. My anxiety mounted as I followed the receptionist to the door of one of the conference rooms, then offered a gracious thank you when she opened it for me to step in.

*Here we go.*

Today, my hair is pulled back into a tight bun, and I skipped the contacts. In my cute black rimmed glasses, bun, and pencil skirt, I was sixty-percent business, forty-percent pleasure, which I could only hope was a good balance. I needed to be enticing, but also taken seriously. Fuck-able, but un-fuck-with-able.

If only Braxton didn't mess with my senses.

He looked even sexier in the light of day. Professional, authoritative, and freaking delicious in the deep blue blazer he wore. I'd hoped that it would take him a second to recognize me in my different persona. No longer the sex-kitten pretending to be a little on the shy side to earn her way up to his room, but the business owner trying to save her livelihood.

But, no.

The way his eyes narrowed as he sat forward in his seat at the head table, he knew exactly who I was, and was wondering what I was doing here.

Showtime.

"Good morning, gentlemen," I said, smiling between him and the two lawyers flanking him. "I don't want to take up too much of your time today, but I'd like to—"

"What are you doing here?"

I flinched as Braxton's voice shot through the air, rumbling through my chest as I inhaled a breath.

"That's what I'm about to explain, Mr. Drake, if you'll let—"

"This paperwork says Michelle Frazier. You're not Michelle Frazier."

Another deep breath.

"I am. Eden Michelle Frazier. I use my middle name for the business."

His eyes narrowed even further, and the lawyers on either side of him glanced in his direction, then at each other before they sat back in their chairs.

"Sit down… Ms. Frazier," Braxton said, and I did.

We were in the same conference room where a little over a week ago, his hands had been on my ass. Now, we sat on opposite sides of a table, opposing sides of an issue. Now, it was just a point of figuring out which of us had the power balance tipped in our favor.

"I own *Ganache*," I started, keeping my voice bright and confident, hoping that it translated to the expression on my face. "If you'll direct your attention to these packets," – I slid them across the table, one for each man, and I had extras – "you'll see that *Ganache* is a full-scale patisserie, speciali—"

"You mean a bakery." Braxton's expression was blank, but the snap in his words told me more than his face could. He was pissed, and I hadn't even drawn the knife yet.

I forced myself to smile. "No. I mean, a patisserie. I have certification as a master pastry chef, so I use that title for my business."

"Okay, *chef*," he said, letting the sarcasm drip over his words as he rolled his eyes. "Why don't you get to the point?"

I swallowed, hard. "Gladly. Late last year, about ten months after I signed a new two year lease, I received a letter from my landlord – Drake Property Management, a subsidiary of Armstrong Hotel Group. That letter was sent to the surrounding business owners as well, to gauge my interest in cancelling my lease. But I wasn't interested, so I declined. Two months later, we got another letter, offering us money to leave. Several of my peers accepted that offer, I did not. Two months after that, another letter, offering more. More of my peers accepted that offer. I did not. I'm the last in the block of buildings. Four months ago, I received a letter stating that my lease would be terminated, and that I had six months to vacate the building before demolition began."

Braxton lifted an eyebrow. "And?"

I glared at him. "*And,* that's not okay! I have sent letter after letter, asking for reconsideration, offering proposals, begging you not to take my business away, and all you have for me is… '*and?*'"

"I haven't seen any of that," Braxton shrugged.

I sat up a little straighter, as a tiny beacon of hope shot through me. "You didn't receive any of my correspondence, from Michelle Frazier?"

"Oh, I'm sure it was *received*, Ms. Frazier." He smirked, and my little bit of hope dropped out of the sky and hit the ground. "I said I didn't see it, because this is a business, and we don't respond to emotional pleas. My lawyers knew better than to even bring it to my attention."

At their mention, both lawyers bobbed their heads, like puppets on screens, and I rolled my eyes, then turned my glare back onto Braxton. "So I've been busting my ass to get you sales reports, recommendations from community leaders, whatever, and you're telling me you didn't even look at it? At any of it?"

Again, he shrugged. "Even if I had, Ms. Frazier, the answer would have been no. This property is the future site of my flagship hotel, right in the heart of the city. My lawyers are in place to make sure that every aspect of this is handled above board, so you'll have to excuse me for taking your word over theirs. It's not negotiable, despite your efforts with your letters, and proposals, and… your body."

My cheeks heated as the lawyer's eyes went wide, then

shot back and forth between me and Braxton. Where I'd felt desire in their stares before, now, with two little words, Braxton had painted a different picture than what they saw before them. Now, they looked with open lust.

"You think I slept with you to gain that kind of currency in this meeting?" I asked, not bothering to hide the disdain in my voice. "Like I thought my pussy was so good you'd just come all over yourself at the opportunity to honor my lease?"

My eyes were on Braxton, but I knew the other men's mouths were open in shock over my sudden shift in demeanor. Braxton, on the other hand, seemed unfazed, and kept his mouth pulled into a smirk.

"That certainly seems to be the case. But... unfortunately..."

"Right," I nodded. "Not convincing enough? Okay. What can I do to convince you?" I asked, leaning forward over the table in a way that made my cleavage look like it was on the verge of spilling from my shirt.

He smiled. "Nothing."

I ran my tongue over my bottom lip, then pulled it between my teeth. "Let me try."

*Got him.*

Braxton shifted in his seat, and I didn't have to be close to know that my innuendo was making him hard. He stared at me for a long moment, then glanced at the lawyers on either side of him.

"Get out," he said, and I didn't move, because I knew he wasn't talking to me. The other two men scurried out, and I stood. I put a little extra *oomph* in the sway of my hips as I rounded the table to reach him.

"Braxton." My tone oozed sex as I stopped in front of him, giving him a lie of a smile that promised everything. "Now, you had lawyers in here, so I'm sure you understand that my lease is a legally binding agreement. I don't care what they told you, I still have time on my lease. What you're doing, trying to force me out… it's not okay."

He grinned. "So… sue me."

"I don't want to sue you. I want you to do the right thing."

"It's *my* building. I own it."

"And I signed a lease!"

"You didn't sign it with me." Braxton sat back in his chair. "I didn't sign any new leases, because I knew what I wanted the building for. You were already a tenant when I bought it."

I threw my hands in the air. "That doesn't change anything! My lease is still valid for almost another year, but going by that letter, I only have two more months before I have to leave."

"So, again, Ms. Frazier – you can sue me, or you can pack up. The choice is yours."

I wanted so badly to smack that stupid smirk off his face. He knew that if I could afford to sue him, I would have already taken action, and his lawyers would be talking to mine, instead of me talking to him. Asshole.

"You said something earlier about doing something a little more convincing," Braxton said, raking his eyes over my body in a way that made me feel naked, and despite my anger… turned me on a little. "You can try that."

I smiled, then reached across the table for the electronic tablet I'd brought in with me. "Mr. Drake… I think that's a good idea."

I turned it on, navigated it to a certain folder, and placed it in front of him on the table, waiting for his examination. He scoffed, then shook his head as he picked up the tablet, but then his eyes bucked wide.

"What the fuck?! Is this—?"

"Your private banking information? The account and routing numbers to access all the money you have in the world? Why, *yes*, Mr. Drake. It is. And this might be interesting too," I said, bending over him to swipe the screen to another page. "Those are private emails, discussing some pretty embarrassing family secrets, business dealings that are legal, but a little on the morally reprehensible side, stuff like that. Oh, and *this*," – I swiped again until I reached the pictures – "these images of your brother in law screwing a woman who is very clearly not your sister... I wonder how Nashira would feel, knowing that you knew about this and didn't do anything?"

Before my common sense could kick in, and tell me to get my ass back, Braxton was out of his seat, bearing down on me, nostrils flared. "I did fucking do something, I paid his bitch ass to leave her alone, and she already knows about it."

"What a good big brother you are," I shot back, standing tall, keeping my eyes on his even though I was terrified. "Too bad you couldn't be a clean businessman too. What you're doing to me isn't right and you know it."

He chuckled, but it had such a bitter edge that it made me flinch. "You stole my private information, and you want to tell me about clean business practices?"

"I tried to do it the right way, with no results, so here we are. I didn't screw you so you wouldn't evict me, I screwed you so I could get access to your computer, and teach you the lesson that you shouldn't let strangers fix your drinks. Are you going to honor my lease or not?"

"Honor your lease? You *broke* your lease by stealing from me, and did you just admit to putting something in my drink? You won't be able to run your business from jail anyway. I'm calling the fucking police, are you crazy?"

This time, I smirked, propping my hands on my hips. "Good luck proving I did anything."

"Luck? I've got the evidence right – what the fuck?!" he said, looking down at the tablet still in his hands. His outburst was caused by the fact that the tablet was now showing a bright red screen, with the words "Game Over" flashing in white. I'd know it wouldn't work for him when I handed it to him, because Willow was controlling it remotely. I'd have to talk to her about taunting him with that Game Over screen though.

"Yeah, the police aren't going to be able to do anything with that. So, back to my point, you can honor the terms of the lease I signed, or the world is going to know all of your shit."

Our eyes met, and the rage I saw in his made it nearly impossible not to back down from his glare. I didn't *think* he would physically harm me, but I wasn't stupid enough to think it wasn't plausible.

"I'm not doing a goddamned thing. Demolition begins in two months."

I swallowed hard, as tears pricked my eyes. "I'll give you time to think about it, before you ruin your reputation and embarrass your whole family because you're pissed off."

I turned away, willing my hands not to shake as I gathered up my documents. I'd worked *so* hard to put all of that together, trying to communicate, trying to get him to see reason. Trying to save the business that meant everything to me.

And it wasn't that he'd examined everything and determined he wanted to screw me over anyway. He'd decided without even looking. No wonder he didn't recognize my name or face that night. I wasn't a valuable business, a person, or even a number to him. I was nothing.

So, fuck him.

"You're not going to get away with this, Ms. Frazier."

I cringed when I felt him right behind me, but I didn't turn around. I finished gathering my things. "Mr. Drake, if anything happens to me, know that there are already contingencies in place that will ensure the release of what I showed you. In case I were to have an accident or anything."

I left one of my folders on the table, then maneuvered away from him, and without another look in his direction, I was out the door.

>> ||| <<

"Welcome to *Ganache*! Would you like to try one of our signature macarons?"

I smiled at the bubbly greeting from one of the cashiers as she recognized me coming through the front door. The sweet smells of cake, chocolate, and cream blended themselves in the air, creating an aroma that made my mouth water, but sat heavily on my stomach, which was still knots. Instead of my normal routine of stopping to speak to the customers, I settled for a friendly wave as I hurried through the shop and into the back.

In my office, I dropped my ignored proposals onto my desk, then held on to the edge as panic gripped my chest again. Even if I did actually go through with releasing his information, it didn't mean anything. We'd *both* just be screwed.

I closed my eyes, willing my heart to stop racing. Two months to pack up a business I'd poured everything into for the last five years, and I'd done everything I could do. Maybe Braxton would show me mercy? No, that wasn't the right way to put it. He'd already denied me mercy, right to my face, so the threat of embarrassment to his family, losing money, ruining business relationships... maybe that would deter him.

Or maybe not.

Maybe he wasn't afraid of that. Maybe he didn't really care. A place in the family business *had* been forced on him, based on the profile Willow and I had put together, developed from the treasure trove of information on him we'd dug around and found. Braxton was smart, and business-minded, but he was also a bit of a wild child. There was a reasonable chance that he would wait me out, or move up the demolition to give me even less time, or… hell, I wouldn't be completely shocked if he hired some shady character to break my kneecaps on principal, not caring if I released the info like I'd said.

He was a wild card.

But I had to *try*.

My cell rang, with the tone I'd reserved just for Willow, who'd been my best friend in the world since I knew what a friend was. Damned near my sister. Still, I wasn't in the mood to tell her yet that Braxton had essentially told me to fuck off, even though she'd probably seen the entire thing on camera.

The phone stopped ringing, and I let out a relieved sigh, still standing with my head bent toward the desk. My stomach was finally calming down, lessening the chance that I would puke, but then it rang a second time.

Willow again, and it had to be bad for her call twice.

*Shit.*

"Hey Will," I said, after digging the phone from my purse. "What's going on?"

She sounded out of breath as she answered. "Braxton Drake just walked—"

"Put the phone down."

A chill ran up my spine at the sound of Braxton's voice right behind me. Willow was still yammering away, her voice squeaking at me from the phone's speaker as I pulled it away from my ear. I turned to face the door, and Braxton pulled it from my hand, hitting the button to end the call before tossing it behind me onto the desk. The loud clatter as it smacked the hard wood broke me from my trance.

"What are you doing here?"

His eyes were narrowed as he backed me against the desk, then put his hands down on either side of me, trapping me in place. "Checking in on my building. That a problem? I can drop in at any time, according to the terms of our lease."

"It's not a problem," I said, hating myself for the tremble in my voice. "We take good care of things around here, and I have nothing to hide."

"We'll see about that."

I dropped my gaze, squirming in the heat emanating from his body. He smelled so damned good, and he wasn't wearing the blazer he'd had on in the meeting anymore. Just his shirt and tie, which was, somehow, even sexier. We weren't touching, not exactly, but his presence, his smell… "Move, plea—"

"Why didn't you just take the fucking money, like everybody else? It was enough that you could have found another place for your business, and moved on." He spat that out like I hadn't even been speaking.

"I couldn't move. I… Braxton, listen. My grandmother raised me. She mortgaged her house to send me to culinary and pastry school. Exhausted her savings to help me start this business when I was fresh out of school. In *this* building. We busted our asses cleaning and remodeling and we put everything into this location. Five years worth of memories. When we got the first letter, about cancelling the lease, we laughed. We weren't going anywhere, this was my baby, her grandbaby. When we got the second letter, we laughed at that too, because did you really think it would take so little to make us leave, when our blood, sweat, and tears is in this place? The third letter, offering the most… we considered.

And she made me promise I wouldn't take it, wouldn't sell my business's soul."

Braxton scoffed. "She sounds dramatic as hell. Granny screwed you over."

"Shut up," I snapped, scowling at him. "Right after I refused the last offer, she got sick. Really fucking sick. I put every dime I had, every dime the business had, into hospitals and doctors, but it wasn't enough. We moved to palliative care, and by the time I got the letter about you terminating the lease, she was already gone. Her life insurance went to paying the leftover medical debts. I have nothing, Braxton. I can't take out another loan. I can't afford to fight you legally, so I'm asking you to just do the right thing. At least let me finish out my lease so I can afford to move, and keep my business alive."

He shook his head, then leaned in closer to me, and I leaned away. "Eden, the story about your grandmother is touching, but you don't get to blackmail people into doing the right thing." His hand moved to the zipper on the side of my skirt. "What if I told you that I could pull my security tapes, and make you famous? Let the whole world watch me fuck you on my kitchen counter, unless you agree to not release my private information that you tricked me and stole?"

"I'd say I look good as hell in that video, and my business could use the publicity *and* the money, if you've got a buyer."

Braxton chuckled, then slid my zipper down. "You are ballsy as fuck. You really are a piece of work."

"And you," I said, smacking his hand away from me. "Are a piece of shit if you think I'm going to sleep with you to make this go away. I'm not a prostitute."

"But you do sell cookies, right? So I beg to differ."

My mouth dropped open as I processed what he meant, and then I shook my head. "Seriously?" I asked, laughing because I couldn't help it. "With that corny ass joke, Braxton? Like, for real?"

"Hey," he said, with a shrug as his mouth spread into a grin. "It accomplished my goal."

"Which was?"

"Make a stupid ass joke to break the tension, so I can catch you off guard."

I lifted an eyebrow. "Catch me off gu—"

Braxton grabbed my chin, holding me in place while he kissed the words right out of my mouth. It took my brain a second to register what was happening, and I told myself to push him away, slap him, *something*. Anything except what I *actually* did – lifted my hands to the back of his head to pull him in closer.

I was supposed to hate him for what he was doing, but somehow my body hadn't gotten the message. His tongue probed the seam of my lips, and I opened for him, letting him devour me. I pushed my breasts against his chest, groaning into his mouth when he dropped his hands to grope my ass.

"I'm sick of talking about this shit," he growled when he ended the kiss. My zipper was still down, and it only took a single tug for him to snatch my skirt down my legs. "I need to feel you again."

The cool surface of the desk made me squirm as he picked me up, propping me on top of it. It was arousing, but at the same time, brought me back to my senses. I put my arms out, keeping him back as he reached to take off my panties.

"Wait a second," I hissed, nostrils flared as I squeezed my thighs together. "You can't possibly think I'm going to have sex with you right now!"

Braxton smirked, easily pushing away my outstretched arms to move closer. "The way you let me kiss you just then... I think you want to do it." He ran a finger over the lace top of the garter and stockings I'd worn under my skirt, an attempt to feel sexy and empowered in our meeting – not meant for anyone's eyes but my own.

"I don't."

"Stop lying, Eden. The way I made you come… please. You haven't stopped thinking about it since that night."

I rolled my eyes… but didn't stop him when he spread my legs to step between them. "I think you're getting confused. You're the one who texted me."

"Because I enjoyed you," he said, chuckling as he deftly opened the buttons of my shirt. "I have no reason to pretend otherwise. I want you again." He tugged down the cups of my bra, exposing my breasts to the slight chill in the air. "So I'm gonna have you."

"Arrogant asshole." I whimpered as he dropped his mouth to my chest, sucking my nipple into his mouth. He scraped over it with his teeth, making me arch into him and grab the back of his head.

"Con artist," he shot back, then moved his mouth to my other nipple. With his lips closed around that one, his fingers teasing the other, he reached into his back pocket for his wallet. With one hand, he maneuvered out a condom, then tossed his wallet onto the desk. I unbuckled and unzipped his pants for him, and then with boxers pulled down, condom on, I let him pull my panties away from my body.

"See?" he asked, then used his other hand to grab my chin, pulling me into another kiss. "I knew you were lying. You want this so bad you can't even help yourself. Can you?"

He wasn't gentle with me, but I didn't need or expect that. I gasped as he drove into me, sinking all the way in with one stroke. "Can you?" he asked again, and I wrapped my legs around his waist, pulling him deeper, closer as he moved. I snatched his shirt open, not really caring if I ruined it, because

I just wanted to be able to touch his skin. My fingernails scraped over his chest, then around to his back, then up to his shoulders and around his neck as I pulled myself closer to him.

Braxton didn't move away from me. The intimacy of the position I'd put us in, it didn't make him recoil at all. Instead, he wrapped an arm around my waist, his fingers digging into my hip as he held me close. He matched the rhythm of his tongue to the rhythm of his strokes, deep, unhurried movements that I could only guess were meant to sear his presence in my psyche, and burn the feeling of him further into my memories.

He was doing a damned good job.

His mouth moved down to my neck, sucking and biting as he buried himself as deep as he could go. The feeling of him, heavy and hard inside of me was incredible, skating the line of pleasure and pain as he pumped faster, harder, until my legs began to shake around him. When the orgasm hit me, I sank my teeth into his shoulder so I wouldn't scream, dug my nails into his back as I clenched around him. The raspy groan he left out when he came shortly after only made my thighs tremble more.

We stayed there on the desk, stuck together, until the pounding in our chests had calmed. I pointed to the bathroom connected to my office when he asked, then climbed down off my desk to pace the floor.

What the hell was my problem?

When Braxton came out of the bathroom, I didn't look at him. I gathered my skirt, grabbed my phone, and went into the bathroom myself, waiting by the door until I heard him leave. A second later, the door opened again, and the distinct sound of high heels clicking across the floor met my ears. I opened the bathroom door to see Willow standing on the other side, a wide grin on her face.

"Told you to be worried, didn't I? That man has you turned out."

>> ||| <<

*I* needed something stronger than wine.

I'd looked at my financial situation, and even if I *was* allowed to stay in my building until the end of my lease, moving would suck my pockets drier than they already were. The profits from those extra few months in the building, plus the tiny little savings account I'd managed not to touch so far would have to keep me afloat in the interim between closing one location and opening another. I could start leasing the new place before the old one closed, but that meant paying rent, utilities, and supply costs for two locations, not to mention staffing both locations.

How the hell would I afford *that*?

And if I didn't get the extra time, if I really did have less than two months to pack up and get out? I was beyond screwed.

So… yeah, wine wasn't cutting it.

I'd looked at my numbers, and had a glass, then had another. Looked at the numbers one more time, and then I finished off the bottle. Willow could have fixed my financial problem in a matter of a few keystrokes, but that was just further towards the moral low ground than either of us were willing to go. We drew the line at blackmail, which, before all of this happened, was further than either of us were willing to go. Maybe everybody has a tipping point where that line gets blurred though. Maybe if Braxton *did* go through with the demolition, I wouldn't release his all of his private information. Maybe I'd just have Willow siphon a few million from him instead, and go live somewhere tropical.

A girl can dream, right?

And speaking of dreaming, no matter how hard I tried, I couldn't get Braxton off my mind. It was like he was constantly at the edge of my thoughts, and at night, my dreams were saturated with him. His smell, the taste of his lips, the feel of him, the sound of his voice, his... everything. Braxton was soaked into my senses, and for whatever reason, I couldn't shake him loose.

I hadn't even seen him, either. I'd forced myself not to internet stalk him, even though it wasn't like that did much good when Willow and I had memorized every stitch of detail about him. His birthday, his shoe size, his favorite food, and even what cologne he liked to wear. We knew the first word he spoke, the first girl he kissed, and the day he got his driver's license, and drove by himself for the first time. All of his information had been carefully gathered, scraped from the internet and any private records Willow could get her hands on. We knew everything about Braxton except the most important thing.

What *really* made him tick? What the hell was going on in his head? And why the hell couldn't I get him out of mine?

Sleeping with him had been a mistake. Never before had a man gotten into my head, without me being able to at least figure out why. I'd slept with people I shouldn't have before, more times than I cared to remember, but something about this was different. Something about him, something about the sex, made me feel connected in a way that I shouldn't to a man who was, essentially, a stranger. Though it was good – incredible, even – just sex, with someone I barely knew, shouldn't have been enough to have my mind gone.

And yet... it did.

Evidenced by the fact that I'd allowed Braxton to fuck me

on top of my desk in my office, not even an hour after a meeting where he'd basically told me he didn't give a shit that he was ruining my life. He'd stood his ass in my office and brushed off my appeal for my business like he didn't matter, and I'd opened my legs and welcomed him, because I wanted him too bad not to. And even though I was just barely past the pleasant soreness from that little desk escapade a few days ago… I wanted him again, so bad it made my head hurt.

But, no.

No, no, no.

That was over.

I had to erase this shit from my mind, at least for one night.

I took a hot bath, and refused to think about him, or money. Made myself a mug of vanilla chai, and refused to think about him, or money. Settled in front of the TV, ready to binge watch some shows, and refused to think about him, or money.

So of course, he knocked on my door.

I was only vaguely surprised when I glanced through the peephole and saw him standing there. I told myself I was only opening the door because I wanted him to stop knocking, but we all lie to ourselves sometimes, right?

"Hey," he said, shooting me a grin when I opened the door.

How dare he stand in my doorway looking this damned good?

The times I'd seen Braxton in person, he was wearing the hell out of suits that probably cost the same as a month of my rent. Braxton in a suit was delectable, but Braxton in a blue tee shirt that stretched across his chest and biceps and sneakers, and dark washed jeans that sat low on his hips… goddamn it.

I swallowed hard, then gave a slight shake of my head, trying to restore my senses. "What do you want, Braxton?"

"To come in."

"You aren't invited."

Braxton took a step back, clutching his chest with one hand like he was wounded. "Damn, that hurts. But… you owe me anyway."

I lifted an eyebrow. "How exactly do you figure that?"

A smile crossed his face again, and he stepped forward, stopping in front of me like he was completely confident I would move aside. "Well, you roofied me, Eden. Remember that? I think the least you could do is give me a few minutes of your time."

Oh.

Okay.

… That was a fair point.

I stepped aside, crossing my arms to hide the fact that his close proximity had made my nipples hard. As he moved past me, into my apartment and I closed the door behind him, I suddenly grew super self-conscious about how I looked.

My hair was still damp from washing and detangling, and I'd pulled it into a bun on top of my head. My breasts were unsupported and unrestrained under the tank-top style sleep shirt I was wearing, and I was reasonably sure my areolas were visible through the thin white fabric. My contacts were in their solution in the bathroom, so I had on my glasses – the better to see my chipped toenail polish with.

*Shit, shit, shit.*

At least I was clean, and not ashy.

The silence between us as I waited for him to speak wasn't necessarily awkward, but it still made me anxious. What the hell was he doing here? And more importantly… why had I let him in?

"Here," he said, holding out a folder that had been tucked

behind his back. I stared at it for a long time before I took it from him, and flipped it open.

"What is this?" My throat went dry as I scanned the pages of legal documents.

He shrugged. "Those are document stating that the terms of your lease will be honored, so long as you promise to destroy the private data you stole from me. There's also a non-disclosure agreement, barring you from talking about that information, putting it in a book, giving interviews about me and my family. None of that."

A tiny gasp escaped my throat, and my lips remained parted as my eyes swept over the words. I wasn't a lawyer, but with my limited knowledge, even I knew that the pages seemed to say what he claimed they did. "I… wh… *what*? Really?" I asked, blinking back a sudden rush of tears that threatened to flow free. "You're not going to… have some-body break my legs, or destroy the building while I sleep?"

"*What?*" Braxton chuckled, then shook his head as he pushed his hands into the pockets of his jeans. "I'm not a damned mobster, Eden. Or a monster."

"Could've fooled me."

"Oh come the fuck on." He scowled at me. "That's not fair, coming from somebody who slipped me a mickey."

I cringed. "Will you stop saying that shit?"

"It's the goddamned truth!"

"I *know*," I said, said, lifting a hand to scratch my eyebrow as I tucked the folder against me, covering my chest. "That's why I want you to stop saying it. I don't feel good about that, about any of this. I was just–"

"Doing what you thought you had to do. I get it. But understand that I really didn't know about this shit. I told my lawyers I wanted the buildings empty, so I could build my hotel. I was on their asses about getting it done, so they used a fucked up tactic, and they mischaracterized the situation to me, which is why I went so hard with you. I already thought you were trying to get over on me, then I find out about the blackmail, and... yeah. Wasn't pretty. But I'm a man of my word, and not into breaking contracts just for the fun of it. Finish out your lease, and we'll just shift the hotel build back."

Warmth flooded my chest, and I swallowed hard, trying my best not to burst into tears. "So... since you're feeling generous, maybe we can put like... another year on that lease?"

"*Hell no*," Braxton said, sucking his teeth. "I'll honor your current lease, but I'm not doing any extra time, are you crazy? This shit is costing me money."

My eyes went wide. "Okay, okay. Just thought I'd ask."

"No."

"Yeah, I gathered that."

Braxton shook his head, but there was a playfulness in his eyes as he pulled a pen from his pocket, clicked it, then held it in my direction. "Alright, so let's get this thing signed."

That time, I was the one who scoffed. "Negro you must be crazy if you think I'm about to sign this right now. I'll give it to Willow to look over, make sure everything is legit first. For all I know there could be something in here requiring me to be a sex slave or something."

"Your pussy isn't all that."

I rolled my eyes. "Whatever, fool. You couldn't wait to get your dick out the other day in my office, and you probably think you're about to get some now. You could've called, emailed, sent this to me via courier, but you didn't. 'My pussy isn't all that', but you're standing in my apartment, hoping I let you put your face in it. Yeah, right."

Braxton's lips were parted, his face pulled into an expression that was half-amused, half shocked. He seemed almost frozen, but then he swiped his face with his hand. "You know… I really like you," he said, shaking his head as he chuckled.

My heart skipped a beat. "What?"

"I said I liked you," he shrugged. "That mouth of yours… you're ballsy as hell, you know that? You manipulated your way up to my room and onto my dick, drugged me, and hacked my computer to save your business. You don't let yourself get pushed around, and it's a turn-on. One of the only reasons I didn't just call the police on your crazy ass."

I chewed at my bottom lip. "One of?"

He nodded. "Yeah. The other is that I had a feeling you were serious about releasing that information, and I didn't want that shit about my sister coming out. Me and my brother had already been working on that, and keeping her protected. I don't want any embarrassment for her if we can help it."

I smiled, and that warmth in my chest blossomed a little more. "You must really care about her, to let my… unfortunate lapse in character slide."

"Oh yeah. Nashira is my whole heart, until somebody else comes to claim some. But… unfortunate lapse in character?" He lifted an eyebrow.

"Yeah," I nodded. "You don't think I make criminal activity a habit, right?"

He smirked. "I don't know, you were pretty damned slick with it. But I'll take your word for it." He pulled the folder from my hands, tossing it onto my counter with the pen before he wrapped his arms around my waist, pulling me close. "Since we're done with that now though, how about we—"

"Uh-uh," I said, quickly squirming my way out of his arms. That little warm feeling in my chest wouldn't go away, and I knew myself enough to know that sleeping with him while I was feeling emotional would be an even bigger mistake than the first two times. "I'm just not... I'm not down for that. Not tonight."

Braxton's expression was thoughtful as he nodded, and I turned away from his gaze. It felt too much like he was stripping me bare with his eyes.

"So what *are* you down for?" he asked.

"Excuse me?"

He chuckled. "What are you down for? What do you want to do? What were you doing before I got here?"

"I don't... I... watching TV, I guess."

"Okay, so let's watch TV."

I watched, dumbfounded, as he kicked off his shoes and sat them by the door, then strolled over to my couch and sat down.

"You coming?" he asked, looking comfortable as hell as he kicked his feet up on my ottoman.

My feet began moving of their own volition, carrying me to the couch, and I... I settled against his side.

*What the...?*

"I like these," Braxton said, after about five minutes of silence had passed between us, while we both pretended our attention was on the TV. Or maybe I was the only one pretending, because the whole time, his eyes had been on *me*.

I started to ignore the fact that he'd spoken, but his gaze was too heated to ignore. "You like what?"

He ran a finger along the thick black frame of my glasses. "These. When I saw you in the conference room that day, in that damned skirt, doing the whole sexy librarian thing... I wanted to bend you over and snatch that skirt up right there."

I bit my lip, suppressing a moan at the way those words hit me right between the legs. I squeezed my thighs together, then took a deep breath. "So my appearance had the desired effect?"

"Hell yes. I was thinking about being inside you the whole time we were in there. And then, in your office, well… you know what happened there."

"I do," I whispered, shivering as his finger traced the seam of my thighs.

"Tell me why I can't have you tonight."

I met his gaze. "Me not wanting to isn't a good enough reason?"

"It's a reason I'll *respect*, obviously. But I still want to know why."

Shaking my head, I looked away, toward the TV, but didn't watch. "Because. I… because I don't know or understand what's happening between us right now. I don't 'get' why we're not at each other's throats, how you can calmly sit here in my apartment after what I did to you."

"I don't understand what's happening either," he admitted, reclining, with his arms stretched along the back of my couch. "I just know that from the minute I saw you sitting at the bar at the hotel that night, something felt different."

Wow… so he felt that too?

"Something like what?"

"Something like… I don't know. Just different. Good different. And even once I found out the shit you pulled, it didn't go away. Maybe because I… kinda get it."

I turned toward him, absently draping my legs across his lap. "Get it?"

"Yeah." He moved his hand down to my thigh, stroking it as he seemed to consider his words. "When I found out about my brother in law, what he was doing to my sister… I wanted to kill him. If my brother Lincoln hadn't talked me out of it, I would have hired somebody to put a bullet through his head, or I would have done it myself. I was ready to *end a life*, because he hurt her feelings. So, I mean… a little drugging and hacking to save your business doesn't seem that fucking bad, to be honest."

I couldn't help giggling as he continued running his hand up my thigh. "Are you serious?"

"Hell yes. I don't play about baby girl." His expression turned thoughtful again as he gently gripped my leg. "But anyway, I'm going to get out of here, leave you to yourself."

I shook my head, laying a hand on his chest. "You don't have to go." I wasn't sure what made me stop him, when I knew damn well I needed to clear my mind. "I just…"

What I couldn't say was that I was suddenly feeling vulnerable, and scared as hell. That little spark of 'something' he mentioned was a mutual feeling we shared, only intensified by sex that wasn't supposed to feel as intimate as it was. 'Something' had never led to anything except hurt feelings for me, and I wasn't exactly eager to experience that again.

Still…

I parted my lips willingly when he pressed his mouth to mine, and welcomed the warmth of his tongue. He tasted even better than I remembered, kissing me – no, *savoring* me – with a kind of passion that added yet another layer of confusion to my mind. But I didn't want to stop.

Braxton's hands skimmed over my thighs, touching and caressing his way underneath my gown. His fingers slid over my panties, teasing me through the layer of soft cotton. I opened my legs, giving him unspoken access to my body, and by association… *me*. Because the way my body hummed in response to him, how could it not affect my mind? How was I supposed to detach emotionally when he slipped a hand under my panties, and just the simple touch of his warm fingers on my bare skin ignited me, each stroke stoked the flame, building it hotter, and hotter, until I was ready to combust?

How could I not let him have me?

"You are so beautiful when you come," he said, licking his fingers when he pulled them from between my legs. He dipped his head, moving so that he was between my legs. "I've got you. Let me—"

"No."

His eyebrow lifted, and he moved back, unhooking his fingers from where he'd intended to slip my panties off. I swallowed hard, then sat up, pushing him so that he was sitting back against the couch cushions. Straddling his lap, I lowered my head to his, placing a soft kiss against his lips. My hands slipped under his shirt, savoring the smooth hardness under my fingers before I gripped the hem. He raised his arms to help me pull it off him, then relaxed again as I settled against his chest, kissing him, sucking his tongue, biting his lips, as I moved my hands between us.

The textured leather of his belt rasped against my skin as I opened it, then unzipped his pants. "Have you been with anyone else?" I asked, whispering the words against his lips.

He smirked a little. "Does it matter?"

When Willow and I gathered his information, we gathered *all* of it, including his health screenings. He was healthy, free of anything nasty he could pass to me... But that was weeks ago. Now, things could be different.

"If I'm about to do this...Yes."

He narrowed his eyes in confusion, but when I slid down to my knees in front of him, and reached into his open pants, pulling his dick from his boxers, he understood.

"No." He shook his head, and looked me right in the eyes before he answered. "Not since you, I haven't."

It was my turn to smirk then. "But my pussy *isn't* all that, huh?"

Braxton laughed, but before he could say anything in response, my mouth was on him. He groaned as I swirled my tongue around him, lapping him up and enjoying the taste of him. I breathed deep through my nose, with him still in my mouth, inhaling the clean musk of his skin as I bobbed up and down over him.

He moved his hand, burying it in my hair to direct me, but I smacked it away. There was fire in my eyes as I looked up to meet his gaze, sucking hard as I came up to the tip. He lifted an eyebrow in challenge, and I took him in deep, swallowing as I went to overcome the urge to gag.

"*Goddammit,*" he hissed, gripping the edge of the couch tight, but I didn't let up. I swirled my tongue around him again, making sure things stayed wet, sucking him hard, and deep, until he bucked away from the couch. He grabbed a handful of my hair again, and his fingers slid over my scalp as I moved, licking, sucking until he told me he was about to come... and I still didn't stop. I kept him in my mouth, not caring that my eyes were watering, not caring that his grip in my hair was bordering between pleasure and pain. I kept going, and going, and going, and after he released, I sat back, picked up my cup from the table beside the couch, and looked him right in the eyes as I sipped from my tea to clear my throat.

"What was that about?" He groaned, panting as he let his head fall to the back of the couch, staring up at the ceiling.

I giggled, then climbed onto his lap. "Showing you," I said, as I sank onto him, "That you aren't the only one who knows how to please. I can do more with a dick than just take it."

Honestly? It was more about trying to regain some semblance of control. If we were doing this tonight, I wanted him on my terms. I wanted to be the aggressor.

And he let me.

"Show me then, beautiful," he said, giving me a sexy smile that made me clench around him. Instead of fighting me for control, he sat back with his lip between his teeth and enjoyed. I pulled my gown over my head, then gripped his shoulders as I rode him. I moaned, grinding him harder when his hands came up to cup my breasts.

I leaned close over him and he moved a hand up to grab my chin, drawing me into a kiss that would have made my knees weak if I'd been standing up. I stopped moving, sinking onto him and enjoying his tongue in my mouth, then on my neck. He trailed kisses all over my skin, dropping to my breasts, sucking, and kissing, and circling my nipples with his tongue as I started riding him again.

"You feel so goddamned *good*," he muttered against my lips, before he kissed me again, slipping his tongue into my mouth to explore and tease and lick. "Eden fits you well."

I felt his hand between us, and a second later, his thumb was on my clit, and any semblance of a rhythm was gone. I was past the point of caring about control when he brought his hands to my ass, gripping and squeezing and pulling me down harder onto him.

I wrapped my arms around his neck, holding tight as my living room filled with the sweet *smack-smack-smack* of skin on skin. I roll my hips against him, trying to take him deeper, and as soon as the thought crossed my mind, there I was, all the way on him, and it was magnificent.

"*Ah, shit*," he groaned, then grabbed my shoulders so I couldn't move as he surged upward like he was trying to push his whole body into me.

"*Ohhhh, yes, yes, yes, yes, shit, YES!*" I screamed, not really caring who heard me as I came. I dug my nails into his back, still rocking my hips as I clenched around him, meeting him stroke for stroke until he plunged one last time, with a deep growl as he released.

His arms were tight around my waist, keeping me stuck to him. Both of us were slick with sweat and panting as he collapsed back onto the couch, pulling me with him. At first when his hand slid over my skin, I flinched, but then I relaxed against his chest as he stroked my back with soft, soothing circles.

He was still inside of me, and hard again when he grabbed a handful of my hair, gently tugging to get me to look at him. When I did, he brought his hand to my chin and tipped it up, giving me another of those confusingly passionate kisses.

"What the hell are we doing, Braxton?" I whispered, then closed my eyes as he kissed me again.

"That's a good question, Eden. I have no idea what the answer is. But… " When I opened my eyes, he was smiling at me, and moved his hands down to cup my ass again. "We can have a good time finding out… if you're down, that is."

I lifted an eyebrow, and the contagious quality of his smile made me grin back. It wasn't like he was the first – or *worst* – man I'd ever bet my heart on. So…

"Okay. Let's see what happens."

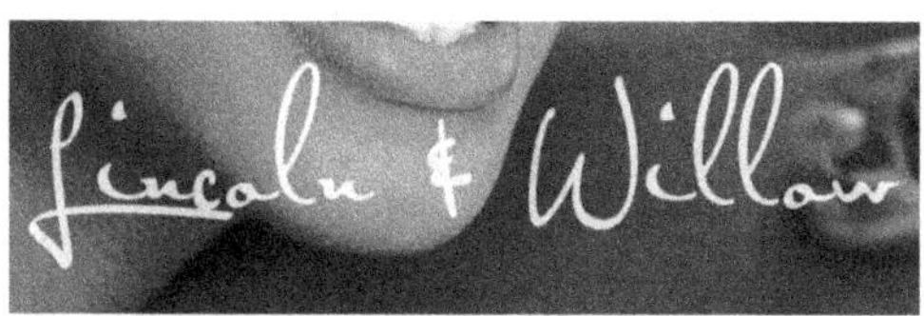

*I*'d have recognized that dick anywhere.

Like… *anywhere*, seriously.

You didn't spend six semi-drunken hours worshipping a dick like that and not *know* it when you saw it. If only I'd known at the time that it belonged to a millionaire… maybe I'd have conducted myself differently afterward. But… I didn't, and now here I was, watching said millionaire make a butt-naked snack run to his kitchen.

I'd just gotten off the phone with Eden, walking her through a little lightweight hacking. All she'd had to do was get the flash drive in the computer, but of course she'd screwed Braxton Drake before she got to it. And I teased her about it, because it was funny, that she'd done *all* of that shit-talking about rich men with wack sex, and then *bam*, life-changing dick.

I hadn't realized I was three doors down from the man who'd given me my own transformative experience. That's how I knew she needed to be worried about it.

Anyway, the party was still going downstairs, and Eden was on her way down the elevator, her hair and dress a mess, but mission accomplished. Once she was out, I would leave my room – one of the junior suites – and get the hell out of there myself. But in the meantime, while I waited on Eden's long ass elevator ride to be over, I entertained myself by flipping through the feeds from the security cameras.

Not the main ones for the hotel. For privacy reasons, those were only in the halls, lobby, etc, the public areas of the hotel. I was looking through the *residence* cameras, the ones that provided security for the family, in the living room, kitchen, balcony, and hall of each suite reserved for their use. And that was when I saw him.

Rich brown skin, poured over a tall, athletic frame. I remembered that body well, hard in the right places, soft in the right places. The fine layer of hair sprinkled over his chest, the slightly thicker trail that led south to pleasure. I remembered how he smelled, all manly and clean, and I remembered how he felt – slightly calloused hands, that lifted and tossed my not-a-size-two ass around with ease.

And like I said, I recognized his dick.

He came into the kitchen with it swinging, and his skin still wet from a shower. He frowned as he looked through cabinet after cabinet and found nothing of his liking, then headed to the fridge. Something about his swagger when he walked felt incredibly familiar, which pricked a memory and made me look a little harder at him. Then he stepped away from the refrigerator with a bottle of orange juice in his hand and lifted it to drink as the door swung shut, leaving me with a perfect view of the front of him.

It was just like I remembered. Heavy, and thick, all one smooth, gorgeous color except the head, and curved a little to the left when it was hard. It was beautiful, and perfect, and made my mouth water a little, and… damn.

I needed to get the hell out of there.

I wiped my gear of anything incriminating, then packed it

into a suitcase with my fake vacation gear and slid it under the bed. Tonight was the opening event, but the hotel had been seeing guests for a week—nobody would think much about me calling to request shipment of a misplaced suitcase.

As I headed out of the room, I cursed myself for choosing my particular heels and dress. I looked damned good, sure, and *needed* to look like I belonged at the party, but damn. The shimmery, jade green, body hugging dress, and sky high heels didn't exactly make for the most practical spy gear.

I mentally thanked the hotel's designer for carpeted halls as I quickly made my way to the door that led to the private service elevator. I punched the button, then checked my phone as I watched the painfully slow ascent from the third floor, which connected to the parking deck.

I was on floor 58.

Eden had made it out of the hotel and was in her car, headed home. Now I just had to get my behind out of there without getting spotted. When the elevator finally arrived, I cursed the loud chime it made and climbed on. I jabbed at the button marked with a three, then pressed and held down the button to quickly close the doors. I let out a heavy, relieved sigh as the doors slid together.

I sucked that breath right back in when a hand appeared in the slight gap in the door.

*Fuck.*

*Just act natural,* I said to myself, plastering a neutral smile on my face as the doors slid open again. And then Lincoln Drake stepped onto the elevator.

I tried my best not to show it outwardly, but my heart started to race. At first, his eyes went wide in surprise at the sight of me, and then sparkled with interest as they swept over me. And I saw it, that little thing I was concerned about, the little thing that could land me in a lot of trouble tonight –

the ghost of recognition in his eyes, even if he couldn't quite grasp why.

"Have to be going somewhere interesting in a dress like that," he said, then glanced at the control panel, not touching it when he saw that it was already going to the third. The doors closed behind him, and he stepped a little closer – but not *too* close – to me. "Were you at the party tonight?"

I shot him a smile, then nodded, while inwardly letting out a sigh of relief that he didn't recognize me. I wouldn't have been able to pick him out of a lineup with his clothes on, so I could only hope the same was true with him for me.

"It was pretty nice, huh? You had a good time?" he asked, pushing his hands into the pockets of his sweats. When I was digging into all the family business for Eden, I hadn't pegged him as a casual kind of guy, but here he was, in sweats and a tee shirt and sneakers, and a nice baseball hat pulled low over his face.

I nodded again, and he smiled at that.

"Good. I went to show my face for a little bit, then I had to break out. Get up to my room, take a shower, *then* realize I don't have any dang food. Real food, not those little snacks and stuff from the party."

The elevator moved past the 31st floor, and I kept my gaze on my hands, my shoes, the doors, anywhere but his direction. He was trying to pull me into conversation, because that was just the kind of man Lincoln was. He wasn't flirting with me, at least not yet. He was just talking.

"You're a guest at the hotel?"

I hesitated over that question, then nodded, because otherwise I would need to explain my presence anywhere beyond the lobby.

"You're quiet, huh?" He said after another few moments passed, then grinned at me. I squirmed under the hot scrutiny of his gaze as the elevator passed the 10th floor. "Well, just so that you know, this elevator is only supposed to be for staff. You can have a pass this time because you look so damned good in that dress."

Okay. So *now* he was flirting.

I blushed, pulling my lip between my teeth so I wouldn't break into a full smile. The elevator passed the 6th floor, and I stepped forward, anxious to get off and get to my car.

"I appreciate that," I said softly, then smiled again, but *his* expression shifted. He narrowed his eyes, and then what seemed like a second later, he was in front of me. The elevator chimed as it stopped, opening the doors to let us off at the third floor, but it had just barely crossed my mind to hurry up and get out when his hand circled my arm.

I held my breath as he leaned closer with a deep inhale, and then his eyes went wide. "It's... it's *you*," he murmured, and my heart dropped to the bottom of my stomach.

"I don't know what you're talking about," I mumbled, shaking my head as I tried to ease away. The elevator chimed again, and then the door closed behind me, confining us into this space.

"I think you do." His eyes were hungry as he advanced, backing me against the mirrored elevator walls. "Your voice... your scent... did you think I wouldn't recognize you?"

I swallowed hard as my back hit the corner, and Lincoln towered over me. "I'm not who you think I am."

"Are you involved with someone?"

"No, I just—*shit*." I whimpered as his hands circled my waist, pulling me against him.

"You're beautiful," he said, brushing a hand through my locs, then bringing it down to cup my face. "Your lips..." I felt it, right between my legs when his thumb skimmed over my mouth. "I remember these lips."

"I don't—"

He swallowed my protest as his mouth covered mine, and the clutch purse I carried clattered to the floor as I fisted handfuls of his tee shirt. His tongue probed the seam of my mouth, requesting entry, and I eagerly gave it. I savored the kiss, giving as good as I got as he teased and explored me. He tasted good. He tasted… familiar.

"You still want to act like you forgot?" he asked, lowering his hands to cup and squeeze my ass. I turned away, but he reached up, shifting my chin right back to face him. "Tell me your name this time."

I shook my head, then whimpered again as his hand ran up my thigh and under my dress.

"I don't tell strangers my name," I hissed, but made no move to stop him as his fingers stroked the thin fabric of my panties.

Lincoln chuckled, then lowered his head to my ear. "That might work if we weren't already so familiar. I've been inside you already," he said, then pushed my panties away. His fingers slipped and slid in my wetness as he eased my thighs apart. "I've tasted you. Felt you come on my dick." He pushed two fingers inside me, then swallowed my moan with another kiss, sucking and biting my lip. "I even came in this pretty little mouth of yours, remember?"

Of course I fucking remembered.

Two years ago, my forays into the dark alleys of the internet had led to the discovery of a well-kept, freaky little secret in my city. A private club, of the type you had to get an extensive background check, sign multiple non-disclosure agreements, and submit to regular, privately conducted infectious disease checks to even be considered.

My curious nature ran too deep *not* to go through the process of becoming a member.

No names exchanged as a general rule. Simple, breathable black silk masks were available and encouraged, so aside from the patrons who were exhibitionists, no faces. Armed security all over the place, and it took *me* two days to hack into their system as a test of their cyber-security. It was safe.

I went, and I observed, thinking there was no way I would ever participate. I didn't tell a single soul, not even Eden, who'd been like my sister since her grandmother took me in as her own, saved me from the foster care system. Not that she would have judged me, I just wanted something that was juicy, and secret, and only for me.

I saw enough that quickly learned what I was and wasn't into. None of the hardcore stuff that went on behind closed doors stirred anything in me. I would burn up the dance floor, and drink at the bar while men and women hit on me, but when offers were made to go to a private room, I always declined.

Until *he* approached me.

There weren't many of "us" in the club to begin with, but he wasn't the first with familiar brown skin to approach me. I gave him the same welcoming smile I gave every other man, and he sat down, and ordered me a drink.

"You have the prettiest lips I've ever seen," he said, and I smiled, knowing that my lips were the only part of my face he could see. "Prettiest skin too, like copper," he added, and I shivered as he took the liberty of touching me. It wasn't anything intrusive, or inappropriate honestly, considering where we were. He slid a single finger down my bare arm, and it set off a drumbeat between my thighs. I knew right then that if he asked me up to a room, I would go with no hesitation.

"Thank you," I said, returning his attention with a soft curve of my lips. "Shea butter and coconut oil to the rescue."

He chuckled. "A natural sista, huh?" And then his hands were in my locs, but instead of feeling groped, or petted like an animal, the soft brush of his fingers made me feel admired.

On most men, the masks we wore to remain anonymous looked kind of silly, but on him, it was sexy... mysterious. The narrow slits in the masks made it impossible to really see his eyes, but as far as I could tell, they were filled with a lust that mirrored mine.

We sat at the bar for over thirty minutes, just talking. No innuendo, and nothing too personal, just... vibing. And he kept touching me. Brushing my locs out of my face, resting a hand on my thigh when he laughed, caressing my shoulder as he ordered us another round of drinks. His touch felt secure, and reverential, and like something I needed to feel in more intimate places on my body. When he leaned close, finally, and placed a kiss just below my ear before he asked me if I wanted to find some privacy, I kept my cool long enough to deliver a quiet acceptance.

My heart raced as he led me through the crowded club and up a set of stairs, to an area I'd never been. The rooms weren't the stereotypically dark dungeons I expected. It was just... a room, with décor that looked like it was pulled right from an upscale hotel.

We didn't waste much time.

The first kiss was exploratory, acclimating ourselves to each other's taste, teasing, and sucking, nibbling and biting, learning what the other liked. The next kiss was more aggressive, his hand wrapped in my locs, the other gripping my ass as he pressed his dick against my stomach. By the time we made it to the third kiss, I was ready to have him inside of me.

But I had to wait.

He took his time to stripping me naked, then spread me over the bed. He kissed, licked, tasted me from my mouth to my toes, then back up, stopping to spread my thighs. He devoured me like a man who was starving, until my legs were useless and weak. He left me on the bed while he retrieved a condom, and then he was inside of me, acquainting me with that curve.

Six hours.

For six hours we made love like we weren't perfect strangers, simply passing in the night. The shower, the dresser, the floor, the bed, licking, sucking, fucking, we did *everything,* until our bodies were spent, and both of us had completely sapped our energy.

Soon, he was snoring, and I lay awake, unable to sleep. My body was still humming with arousal, my heart churning with misplaced passion, and my mind swimming with confused feelings over the fact that the best sex of my life had happened with a stranger.

And I didn't want to leave.

That was a problem. That was *the* problem.

I wanted him still, again and again, and that wasn't supposed to be a thing. This was supposed to be anonymous, to fill a simple need and move on, not the beginning of a fling. A one shot. For all I knew, this man was married – to a woman who knew what he was into, but still – or a criminal, or a *married* criminal, whose wife would find out about this shit and shoot me in the face.

I was way too cute to get shot in the face.

So I got up. I scrambled into my clothes, and strapped on my heels, and I got the hell out of there. And I hadn't been back since, because I didn't want to run into him again.

*Damn you Eden,* I thought to myself, because if it wasn't for her, I wouldn't be questioning the course of my life while pressed into the corner of an elevator, with Lincoln's fingers in me.

"Do you remember?" he asked again.

I wasn't convinced it was a memory that would ever

leave. I even remembered how he'd tasted, warm, and salty and clean, like a man who ate well and drank his water.

*Still.*

I kept my eyes shut, and my mouth shut, hoping this would all fade away into a dream. But no. His hand, gripping and squeezing my ass, was real. His lips on my neck and mouth were real. His fingers, stroking and probing and exploring were real. "See how wet you are for me?" he murmured into my lips. "*She* remembers. *She's* not denying me. *She* is weeping, tears of joy about this little reunion." The way I clawed at his back through his tee, arching myself into him as I came all over his fingers… *very fucking real.*

"*Lincoln,*" I managed to whimper, chest heaving as I tried to calm my breathing.

He glanced at me as he retrieved his wallet from his pocket, then pulled out a condom. "So you know my name, but I can't know yours?"

"It's complicated."

"It's really not," he said, shamelessly dropping his boxers, and rolling the condom on as he reached for me. "We're going to do this right here, because I can't wait, and then I'm going to take you back up to my room, where we'll do it again, and you'll tell me your name."

I shook my head. "No."

"No to… all of it?"

I dropped my eyes, and my gaze landed right on his dick, long, and thick, and curved, and waiting for me. The throbbing between my thighs shot to a level past intense, and I ran my tongue over my lips.

"No to going to your room. No to telling you my name."

"Not good enough."

"It has to be."

I avoided meeting his eyes, and I could feel his hesitation. His shoulders were tense, probably a mix of disappointment and anger, but I didn't flinch when he reached to grab my chin.

He plunged his tongue into my mouth, kissing me slow and deep as he moved his hands down to my ass. He picked me up, wrapped my legs around his waist as he pressed me deeper into the corner, and then he pushed my panties to the side, and plunged into me.

And... *damn*, it was just as perfect as I remembered. My body remembered too, stretching and accommodating to fit him as he stroked me deep. I slipped my hands under his shirt, digging my nails into his back, pulling him closer as he buried himself in me.

"Why are you playing, girl?" he asked, trailing from my collarbone to my ear with his tongue. "You know your pussy was made for me. You said so, remember?"

My only response was a whimper as I bit down on my lip, because fuck him for bringing up those memories.

Yes.

I absolutely *had* said that to him.

We'd been lying together, with me tucked against his side, my thigh draped over his. I'd slid my hand over his chest, down my stomach, and then wrapped my fingers around his dick and stroked. *"This is perfect,"* I'd whispered to him. *"You're perfect. Perfect thickness, perfect length. Like it was made just for me, just for my pussy."* I'd felt bold, and sexy, and perfectly scandalous, and then I'd taken him in my mouth, and we both reaped the benefits of that bold-sexy-scandalous feeling.

My eyes watered with tears of bliss as he filled me, over, and over, and over with strokes that alternated between slow and deep, and swift and deep, and hard and deep. Always, *always* deep. The tingling began in my toes and between my legs, then spread over my whole body. His rhythm became more and more erratic the louder I moaned, the harder I scratched his back, the deeper he plunged into me.

When I came, it attacked my body in waves, filling me with tension that dissipated in a burst of bliss, then came right back, over and over again. When he came, he plunged into me with a rough growl that rumbled in my chest and a stroke that took the last of my breath away. After a few moments passed, he let me down, then grabbed me again to steady me.

My legs were wobbly and weak, just barely holding me up, but I pushed him away, using the handrail for balance as adjusted my panties and pulled my dress back down over my hips. Lincoln was staring at me, and I knew he had something to say, something that would make it even harder for me to get away. But then the elevator chimed, and the doors started opening, and he had to turn away to tuck himself back in.

I snatched my forgotten purse from the floor, then shot past the confused looking valet. My lungs were burning, and I was reasonably sure I'd fucked up my ankle running in my heels by the time I made it to my car, but I didn't waste time tending to either.

I started the ignition, and got the hell out of there.

>> ||| <<

*E*den's bakery – sorry, patisserie – was just across the street from the office space I used for my small internet security business. I didn't really need an office space, but I had it anyway, so I would have a reason to get dressed and feel the sun on my skin during the weekday. I only had a couple – as in, exactly two – employees, but I'd built the business to a place where if I wanted to, I could just delegate the work to them for the day.

Today was one of those days.

A little over a week had gone by since my little… interlude… in the elevator with Lincoln, and just the thought of it made me clench my thighs. The imprint of our rendezvous two years ago had already been irrevocably burned in my mind. Now, after having him inside me again, the feeling was just intensified.

I couldn't even focus on my work. Every time I closed my eyes, my mind went immediately to him. How he felt, and smelled, and tasted. How on that first night, he'd taken the extra – but unnecessary – step of talking to me, making me comfortable first, before he asked me to go upstairs with him. How he had a presence that was confident and authoritative without being domineering and aggressive. How he'd taken control while never making me feel I was being controlled.

How he was so fucking perfect.

But I couldn't do anything with a man like that. A man who, after being with him a grand total of less than eight hours over two years, had my head so messed up I couldn't run my business? No fucking thanks. I was way too crazy for that shit.

I'd busted windows and keyed cars over *mediocre* dick. If I let Lincoln in any further and he screwed me over? There was a good chance I just might kill him.

Those were the thoughts that drove me to my front window, watching people instead of watching the screens. Eden's car was parked in front of her building, which meant she was back from her meeting. I'd helped her earlier, with laying out her little blackmail plan against Braxton, and I hoped beyond hope he would just accept it.

The *last* thing I needed was a Drake hotel right across from me.

Another car pulled into the parking lot, and my heart shot into my throat as the door opened, and long, designer slack-clad legs stepped out. I calmed a little when I saw the facial hair, because Lincoln kept his face clean-shaven.

But...

*Holy shit,* that was Braxton!

I shot back to my desk and grabbed my phone, dialing Eden's number. When she didn't pick up the first time, I called again, just as Braxton pulled open her front door.

*Pick up the goddamn phone,* I screamed in my head, pacing the floor.

"Hey Will," Eden said when she picked up on the fourth ring, sounding drained. "What's going on?"

"Braxton Drake just walked—"

"Put the phone down." I could hear Braxton's voice faintly through the phone, and my "Oh, *shit*!" meter went through the roof.

"Eden, what's going on?! Are you okay? Is he—"

The only answer I got was the melody from my phone telling me the call had been ended.

*Damn, damn, damn.*

I told my staff I was going to lunch, then headed out the door. As I waited to be able to cross the street, I clutched my much-loved key chain tight in my hand. Pepper spray and a pocket knife were the only weapons I had, but I was sure I could grab a rolling pin from the *Ganache* kitchen on my way.

Once I got across the street, I headed right through the front door. I toyed briefly with the idea of destroying that pretty ass car, but that could wait until I was on the way out.

I went straight to the back, stopping to grab that rolling pin before I got to Eden's office. Her door was cracked, just about an inch, and as I listened to their raised voices go back and forth, I played a brief fantasy of catching Braxton off guard and going upside his head for running up on my sister-friend.

But then I peeked through the crack.

Oh.

*Ohhhh.*

Eden's ass was in Braxton's hands. They were still wearing clothes, but with a kiss like that, I wasn't really sure why. And then he pulled her zipper down.

Damn.

Right to business.

I pulled the door closed as quietly as I could, then went back to the kitchen to give the rolling pin back to the confused cake decorator I'd taken it from. And then I waited – honestly longer than I thought I'd have to – for Braxton to come rushing out of Eden's office.

He was in the hall before I knew what was happening, and almost knocked me over. He barely looked at me – and I'm *fine*, okay? – as he grabbed me by the arms to restore my balance. He mumbled an apology and headed out, looked rumpled and smelling like sex.

I grinned as I eased open the door to Eden's office. When I didn't see her at first, I stepped inside, then walked quickly across to the bathroom connected to her office. She must've heard me coming, because she peeked out just as I approached.

"Told you to be worried, didn't I? That man has you turned out," I teased, playfully poking her arm. "In your office, Eden? Really? You know I had to close your door?"

She rolled her eyes. "You've been here the whole time? Thanks a lot for saving me."

"You didn't look like you wanted to be saved."

"All the more reason to do it."

I turned away, but stayed there in the door as she washed herself up. "You needed a little fun in your life anyway," I tossed over my shoulder. "You just ended up getting better than you bargained for. So what happened? Is he honoring your lease?"

"No. I explained everything, even about Nana, and he didn't care."

I scowled. "Seriously? I thought he was probably a little bit of an asshole, but I didn't peg him as heartless like that. Maybe something else is going on."

"You mean like maybe he's pissed about my attempt to blackmail him? Uh, yeah, probably."

Shaking my head, I laughed a little. "You didn't put it on him good enough E. What's a little drugging and hacking and blackmail in the grand scheme of things, really? That's what you should have asked him."

"I need you to shut up."

"I'm being for real. In all seriousness though, do you know he walked right into me in that hall, and didn't even give me a second glance, as good as I look? You messed that man's head up girl."

"Whatever, Will." Eden nudged me out of the doorway so she could step out, looking a little wrinkled, but at least not like she'd been fucked. She sat down at her desk, dropping her head into her hands. "What am I going to do?" she moaned, then lowered her forehead to the slick wooden surface of the desk.

"I don't know," I quipped back, patting her on the shoulder before I headed to the door. "You may want to start by cleaning the desk. Y'all nasty."

I blew her a kiss in response to her raise middle finger, just before I closed the door behind me and left.

She may not have known what *she* was going to do. But I definitely knew what *I* was going to do.

>> ||| <<

My mind had started racing with questions as soon as Lincoln walked through the door of my restaurant. Well… not *my* restaurant, but this was where I came when I wanted good food and good vibes and free wifi that wouldn't be traced back to my apartment, so… it was mine. And as far as I was concerned, he was invading my space.

It didn't help my anxiety that I was currently in the middle of a very casual hack against Braxton, doing a little lightweight "convincing" him to reconsider his decision not to help Eden after that meeting yesterday. His lawyers were being very, very naughty, right under his nose, he just needed a little help seeing it.

Anyway.

What the hell was Lincoln doing *here* anyway? This was a spot in the hood, no Perrier to be found. Had he found out my name? Did he know where I worked? How the fuck did he find me?

I watched him, but pretended not to, as he walked up to the counter. I'd seen him as soon as he came through the door, and he hadn't looked my way, so maybe… maybe this was a coincidence? The city was big, but still small. Just like I'd stumbled upon him in the hotel without looking for him… I guess it could work that he'd just stumbled upon me.

There he was, dressed casually again, just like in the elevator that night. Ordering a plate of fried catfish, okra, green tomatoes, macaroni and cheese and green beans, with a slice of pecan pie, and I think I may have fallen in love with him, based solely on his food order.

Good dick, and he could appreciate a good plate of real – albeit not that healthy – food? Shit just wasn't fair.

I weighed the idea of making a run for it, but decided against it. It would just call more attention to me when he may not have noticed anyway, since I was tucked into a booth in the corner of the tiny diner. And even if I got away, the owner, Mr. Sammy, was always trying to hook me up with somebody anyway. That fool would give Lincoln my name, address, blood type and twitter handle in a heartbeat.

I kept my ass in the booth and tucked my head a little lower.

He sat down at the counter to wait, and as he did, he looked around. I looked away, but apparently not fast enough, because a few moments later, he slid into the booth across from me, and said words it honestly threw me off a little to hear.

"You look familiar."

I scrunched my eyebrows together. What in the world was he… was he *playing* with me? "No, I really don't," I answered back, not looking up from my laptop screen.

His fingers hooked around the bottom edges of my screen, pulling it ever-so-slightly away from me. "You definitely do."

"You're mistaken." I moved the computer back toward me across the table.

"I'm not. A week and a half ago, I saw you at the grand opening of a hotel downtown."

I pushed out a little sigh, then looked over my screen at Lincoln. Sweet Jesus, he was finer than fine. That sculpted jaw, gorgeous smile, and deliciously warm, deep brown skin, just slightly darker than mine. The kind of dark brown eyes you got lost in, instead of looking into. Inwardly, I sighed.

"No you didn't," I said, then forked off another bite from

my own pecan pie. "You're mistaking me for someone else. I wasn't at any grand opening."

Lincoln smiled, then leaned back, relaxing against his chair. "Nah, you're not the type of woman who gets mistaken for someone else. You had on this sexy green dress, and I remember admiring how good it looked against your skin."

I shook my head. "Wasn't me."

"You had your locs down, and your shoulders were bare."

"Definitely not me," I said, with a wry smile. "And I'm waiting on someone, so if you could move along…"

"Waiting on someone like a boyfriend?"

"Waiting on someone like a friend."

"Then they won't be upset about you having a friendly conversation, right? If this person is just a friend."

I let out a hiss of air through my teeth. "What is that you want?"

"I want to know your name."

"No."

He grinned, and I felt the sudden urge to check that my panties were still there, because surely they'd burned right off when he smiled at me like that.

"Fine," he said, holding up his hands in defeat. "I want you to tell me why you won't admit to being the sexy woman in green at the party that night."

"Because it wasn't me," I quipped back, then looked up as one of the food runner's delivered his food and drink. To *my* table. "Um, excuse me… are you really just about to eat here, like it's nothing? I told you I was meeting someone."

Lincoln shrugged. "Okay, so they can pull up a chair."

"I… I…," I couldn't think of anything to say, as he started eating like there was nothing odd about him – a stranger to me as far as *he* knew – randomly sitting at my table and eating with me. He tucked in – like, for real *grubbing* – like I wasn't even there, and then after a drink from his water glass looked up at me with a smile, and winked.

Holy.

Shit.

"So you thought I looked hot?" I asked, in an attempt to throw him as off-balance as he'd placed me.

He ate a few more forkfuls of food, before he looked at me. "I didn't *think* you looked hot. I know you did."

"What do you want from me? Why are you sitting here?"

He cocked an eyebrow. "Answered that already. I want to know your name."

"And I've already said no, and now I'm saying it again."

"So tell me why," he said, then ate a little more. "Explain why I can know your body like the back of my damned hand, but not your name."

I rolled my eyes. "Because it's—"

"And save the bullshit, please. Just give the bottom line."

"Fine," I shrugged. "Because me with you would be like a kitten with catnip. I wouldn't be able to get enough, and you would make me crazy. I'd go nuts. And then you'd fuck up, and I'd go even more nuts, and somebody would be in the morgue, and I don't your family wants to ever have to identify your body, I've heard it's not pleasant at all."

Lincoln's eyes went wide, just before he threw his head back and laughed. "You can't be serious? So, what, you figured out who I am, so you assume me to be some type of playboy. You just already know I'm going to fuck up without giving me a chance?"

"Yes," I nodded, then took a sip from my lemonade. "It's not because I think you're a playboy though, I know for a fact you're not. I have a really long memory, and a really short fuse. I know you're going to fuck up because you're a man, and all men do. My threshold for bullshit is too low to take that risk."

I shrugged, then finished off my lemonade.

"Wait, wait, wait now. Come on, girl. With that ass and those thighs, that face and those lips, looking like you do, smelling you do," – he leaned in a little across the table, with a wicked grin – "*tasting* like you do, with *this* attitude... you're not gonna tell me you've never been the worst fucking thing to happen somebody."

I pulled my lip between my teeth, trying not to smile. "Absolutely not. Maybe once. Maybe... a time or two."

"See there!" He clapped his palms together before returning to his food. "I knew it!"

"Yes, and I did too. Even more reason for you to get up and walk away, and we can let this all remain a pleasant memory. What, you want us to be the worst thing that ever happened to *each other*? Sounds like a match made in hell."

"Or maybe I mellow you out. Maybe I'm your balance. Maybe the reason you've been so easily irritated with other men is because they were trying to complete you instead of complement you, which is what you need. Maybe they just didn't measure up to your expectations because they just... weren't me?"

Why the hell didn't that feel condescending, or arrogant? From any other man's mouth, those words would have made me feel like stabbing something – preferably him – so why was it different coming from Lincoln?

It wasn't like he was... oh hell, there wasn't any way he could be right... right?

"I'm leaving," I announced, then closed my laptop and stuck it in my bag. I tossed a twenty on the table, and was out the door before Lincoln even put his fork down.

That was a mistake. A major mistake, and I knew it, to spend even that much time talking to him. There he was, pulling me deeper, and there *I* was, just letting him, like I didn't know better.

I definitely knew better.

I wasn't surprised when I heard Lincoln's footsteps, approaching me on the sidewalk at a jog. He passed me first, then turned around, so I'd have to walk past him.

"So you're going to stalk me now? I believe in concealed carry, just so you know."

He stopped walking. "I'm not trying to stalk you, beautiful. Just trying to convince you to take a chance. But… I'll let it go, if it's like that."

"See?" I tossed over my shoulder. "You can't handle me. One little threat of a gunshot wound and you're ready to give up?"

Behind me, Lincoln laughed, and a few seconds later he grabbed my hand. "Actually, it was when you used the word 'stalking'. I don't want to leave you with a negative impression of me."

"Oh," I said, trying to ignore the frenzied tingles coming from the hand where he was touching me. "I guess that makes sense. But if you're not stalking me, how did you know to find me here?"

At that question, he smiled. "I… I've actually seen you at Sammy's several times. We were actually born around here, lived here before my mom married an Armstrong. So I come back when I want a little taste of home. Like I said, I've seen you in there, always with your head buried in your laptop. And… looking at you, I felt like there was *something*, but I just thought it was because you were fine as hell."

"Why didn't you approach me?"

"Because you didn't look like you wanted to be bothered. Headphones in, head buried in your laptop… it would have been intrusive, and rude."

I lifted an eyebrow. "But today wasn't?"

"Today, I'd been looking for you for over a week. I took the chance."

I swallowed hard, then nodded. "Right."

"You know that's how I recognized you first, that night? I remembered your face, from the diner. And *then*, when you spoke, and when I got close to you, your scent. That's when I knew you were…"

He trailed off, like he was trying to figure out what so say.

"That's when you knew I was… what?"

"The one who changed everything."

I swallowed even harder then, and tried to ignore the little voice in my head telling me to run before it was too late. "How so?"

"Everybody else is boring now. And boring isn't good enough anymore. Not since you."

Damn.

I should have run when I had the chance.

"I'm a hacker, you know?" I said, pulling my hand from his. "I hacked you. I hacked your brother. I helped my friend steal information that she's going to use against him. That's why I was in the hotel that night."

There was silence as he stood there and stared at me, his eyes narrowed and confused. "Wow… Brax told me about that shit… that… that was *you*?"

I shrugged. "How else would I know about it?"

"*Wow*," he mouthed, then shook his head. "You… weren't lying when you said you were crazy, were you?"

I smiled. "Not even a little."

"So Eden the Badass is your friend?"

"I taught Eden how to be a badass."

Lincoln looked up toward the sky, then chuckled as he dropped his gaze back to me. "I can't wait to tell Braxton how alike we really are. This twin shit is crazy."

"What does that mean?" I asked.

He shook his head again. "Nevermind. Back to you and me. You told me about what you did, thinking it would turn me off, but I actually argued for your friend's side. I thought Braxton deserved it."

I tipped my head to the side. "Really?"

"Yeah, really. So… I'm looking at you on some "fight the power" type of shit. If you're trying to turn me off… you need another approach."

Damn, why couldn't he just give up?

"It takes me a long ass time to wash my hair. Like, hours. And I drip everywhere for a long time after."

"That's the best you've got?"

I pressed my lips together. "You're rich, so if I date you, I'm not paying for shit."

"Why would I expect you to?"

"Because I'm grown, I don't need a man to take care of me."

"Then pay for your own shit."

"No thanks. As I mentioned before, you're rich."

He burst into laughter after I said that, and I couldn't help laughing with him. It felt familiar, and good, and reminded me of that night at the club where we'd laughed and sexed and enjoyed each other for that short time.

Was it even possible to have that long term?

"I may be crazy," I started, walking up to him and standing close enough for our bodies to touch. "But I'm not unreasonable. You turn and walk in the other direction, don't follow me home."

The disappointment in his eyes was clear, but he nodded. "I'll respect your wishes."

"Good." I smiled. "Meet me tomorrow night at eleven… at the club. We can start from there, okay?"

He smiled at me, in a way that made it hard to follow through with this particular plan. Taking him home seemed much better, but I needed to finish my little project with Braxton for Eden, and that took priority.

"I can do that," Lincoln said, with a slight nod. "Does this mean you're finally going to tell me your name?"

I grinned, then pushed myself up on my toes to brush my lips across his. "Nope." I kissed him again, opening my mouth in welcome when he dipped his tongue in. He kissed me deep, with his hands at my waist keeping me against him, and when he finally pulled back, he murmured a quiet "*Why?*" against my lips.

"Because," I said, pulling away with a smile.

I started walking away, then turned around to see him standing in the same spot, hands pushed in his pockets, looking like he'd just had the best day of his life.

"You already know my body through and through, Lincoln. I have to leave *something* for you to figure out.

ABOUT THE AUTHOR

Christina Jones is a budding author on a mission to show the beautiful -- but not always pretty -- journey of love in all stages, with a focus on people of color. When she's not immersed in writing it, Christina is an avid reader of her favorite genre, Black romance.

Read her blog: www.BeingMrsJones.com
Follow her on Twitter: @BeingMrsJones